Girls
9–12 years

£1·00

FERRYMAN'S FOLLY

FERRYMAN'S FOLLY

by

H. P. BENNEY

KINGSWAY PUBLICATIONS

EASTBOURNE

ISBN 0 86065 173 8

Printed in Great Britain for
KINGSWAY PUBLICATIONS LTD
Lottbridge Drove, Eastbourne, E. Sussex BN23 6NT by
Fakenham Press Limited, Fakenham, Norfolk

CONTENTS

CHAPTER ONE

EXPRESS ADVENTURE

The adventure began on Paddington Station. At least this was the particular bustling London terminus where one memorable July Thursday Ann and Brian Kent first bumped into the Enemy. It was Brian, of course, who did the actual bumping. Bumping into things and people was something Brian did a lot of, especially when he happened to be absorbed in anything as fascinating as the latest issue of *Zoom-man Comic*. Brian had, in fact, just reached that nerve-twitching stage in the week's episode where Zoom-man was about to wrestle single-handed with the seven-headed Zworg of Zwandra in his heroic bid to rescue the lovely Llana from the monster's clutches, when the inevitable happened.

Boys like Brian just cannot wander through crowded railway stations at holiday time, their heads buried in comics, without inviting disaster of one kind or another. Disaster on this particular day took the form of an untidy-ginger-head-into-neat-waistcoat collision which sent the Enemy staggering backwards over a jumble of luggage, arms flapping, completely off-balance. Of course, at that particular moment in time neither Ann nor Brian realised that this long, thin gentleman, who by now lay sprawled on his back in a heap of assorted holiday cases, actually was the Enemy. That knowledge would come later. But even this early in the adventure the impending explosion of anger building up behind the thin-rimmed glasses seemed to suggest that here was a man who could not actually be counted a friend.

All innocent eyed, Brian lowered the now rather crumpled comic and stared open-mouthed at his spread-eagled victim.

"You all right, mister?" The anxiety in Brian's voice was more for his own safety than for his victim's state of health.

The explosion came. The Enemy had a thin, harsh voice, which seemed completely in tune with his thin face, thin pointed nose and gaunt figure. In fact, everything about the Enemy seemed harsh and thin, particularly at that first meeting, as Brian —veteran of a thousand tickings off though he was—wilted under the tirade of fury from his indignant victim. By the time Ann came hesitantly to her brother's aid, the Enemy had vented his wrath, dusted off his black business-suit, snatched up his thin, black business-case and stalked away into the milling crowds, with Brian's recently purchased *Zoom-man* thrust under his arm. Brian stood slightly dazed, with expressions like 'long-haired lout' and 'ill-mannered youth of today' still ringing in his ears.

"Stealing, that is," he was muttering. "Taking someone's comic."

"Deserved it, didn't you?" fussed Ann, who was still blushing at the embarrassment of her brother's behaviour. She had reached the age where blushes came easily.

"What you mean?" protested Brian, his eyes shining with shocked indignation. "Didn't you see that? He took me comic—stole it, he did!"

"Serves you right for not looking where you were going," scolded Ann. "Come on. The train leaves in five minutes. I told you to hurry back when you went to buy that silly comic. If I hadn't come looking for you, I don't know where you would have ended up." She snatched her brother's hand and began dragging him towards the ticket barrier. Taking her brother on holiday was not proving as easy as her mum had promised it would. "You can't go wrong, Ann, love," had been Mrs Kent's final words, as she waved them goodbye at East Croydon Station. "You know your way round the Underground and you're old enough now to find the right train at Paddington. Just keep a firm hand on Brian, that's all."

'All' was to prove a small word for the responsibility of looking after a boy as spirited as Brian. On the fast journey into Victoria from East Croydon it had taken the combined efforts of three burly workmen to haul the boy back into the carriage after he had almost disappeared out of the train window. On the Circle Line, which connects Victoria with Paddington, the mainline station to the West Country, Brian had somehow managed to get his coat jammed in the automatic doors of the Underground train. Eventually it took 20 amused passengers and one distinctly unamused guard to free him and so allow the train to complete its journey. The collision episode was just another link in a growing chain of embarrassment which threatened to turn Ann's eagerly awaited holiday into something approaching a nightmare.

"Leggo, girl," he was protesting, as she dragged him back towards the Penzance express. "Just let me nip back to the magazine kiosk and buy an-uvver *Zoom-man*. You can't expect me to get on that train without finding out what happens next."

"No time," insisted Ann, firm-lipped and without mercy. "The train's about to go."

"Help me, mister. I'm being kidnapped," he squealed, as his sister dragged him past a grinning ticket collector. But all his protests were in vain and Ann persisted in her determined 'kidnapping'. Sleek and powerful, the great express stood poised for her flight to the sand and sunshine of the Cornish Riviera. Ann sighed with relief as she reached the carriage where she had already stowed their cases. It was the coach immediately behind the streamlined diesel engine which stood frowning down the tracks, impatient to be off and burning up the miles to that holiday playground in the extreme south-western tip of England.

A rather dignified old lady sniffed and drew herself back into the corner of the carriage as Brian came bounding through the door and flopped down into the seat alongside her. The elderly gentleman in the opposite corner glanced over the top of his paper and sighed softly before grunting to his feet, easing down his case from the overhead rack, and setting off along the corridor to find some more peaceable carriage. The old lady was of sterner stuff. Setting her jaw grimly, she fished into an enormous raffia bag at her feet, produced a jumble of wool and needles, and proceeded to apply herself to the task of knitting. By the time a cheer from Brian and a shudder from the carriage announced the start of the journey, she was busily clicking in fine style. Ann, her face still slightly pink, sat silent in a corner as far from Brian as she could get, and tried to pretend that he was not her brother at all.

"Not often we travel by train," offered Brian after a while. The old lady ignored him. Under her breath she was muttering something about plain and pearl. "Mostly we go places by car," continued Brian undaunted. "Dad's got a mini—bit of a squeeze it is, but cheap on petrol." The old lady was obviously not a bit interested in the motoring problems of the Kent family and continued steadily with her knitting, oblivious to the boy's idle prattle.

As the express rattled out through the drab suburbs of Greater London, Ann closed her eyes and let the sight and sound of Brian drift far away. She was going to enjoy this holiday in Cornwall. This was the very first time the two children had ever gone on a holiday without their mum and dad. This year, Ann's parents had decided to forgo the annual holiday and to spend the time redecorating the house. The problem, of course, was Brian. What was to be done with him? Mr Kent shuddered at the thought of Brian bounding about all the school holidays between tins of paint and buckets of wallpaper paste. His wife shared this trepidation and immediately sat down and wrote letters to every relation she could think of, almost pleading with them to take Brian and his sister for a month in July and August.

" 'Course I could help," Brian had muttered, a little peeved at this anxiety to get him out of the way. "I expect I'd be awful good at painting and stuff. You ought'a see me in art at school."

But Mrs Kent had received tearful letters from teachers about Brian's activities with a paint-brush at school, and the memory only confirmed her resolve to get her offspring well out of the way while the house was being painted. Unfortunately, most of the Kents' relations knew all about Brian, and back bounded polite letters offering shallow but firm excuses against taking the children. The only relations who had never met Brian were Uncle Joseph and Aunt Jocelyn, who lived in far-off Cornwall, and it was only from this quarter that a favourable reply dropped through the letter-box of the Kents' Croydon home.

Cornwall. Ann let the flavour of the word linger in her mind. Somewhere near the sea her aunt and uncle lived. The letter had mentioned something about boats and swimming. Even the address had been intriguing! Ferryman's Folly, Gill Creek, near Truro. And now here they were speeding on their way by powerful diesel towards that delight-ful-sounding spot. The journey seemed much longer than Ann had imagined it would be. The minutes crept into hours as the green landscape of the approaching south-west unwound past the window. Drifting fields, half-glimpsed villages, flashing telegraph poles, a whole world they could never explore passed by on the other side of the carriage window. The initial wild excitement of the journey died, and with the rhythmic clack of the train wheels and the steady click of the old lady's knitting needles there came a dull boredom which seemed to seep slowly into the bones of both children.

At first Brian fidgeted and complained, and it took all Ann's determination and guile to prevent his slipping out of the carriage and going on an adventure tour of the corridor. But now he sat, his sulky eyes half closed, cheek resting against the cool carriage window, looking for all the world like one bored little boy. Anyone who could have peered into his thoughts, however, would have been in for a shock, for at that very moment Brian was saving the train from a terrible disaster. *The diesel driver had been struck down in his cab by a poisoned dart fired from a passing bridge. The dreaded Wong Gang were at work. But fortunately Brian was at hand to foil their dastardly plans. Although the express was now hurtling uncontrolled towards a wrecked viaduct where they would all be plunged into some deadly torrent hundreds of feet below, Brian had scrambled out onto the roof of the train and, agile as a cat, ducking to miss the low bridges as they flashed by, he had leapt lightly across to the engine. With the smashed viaduct almost on them, he quickly repaired the damaged brakes. His hands were tense*

*on the controls as the hurtling express screamed
to a halt—just inches short of the crumbling edge
of the viaduct* . . . Brian mopped his brow.

He glanced out of the window. The train *was*
slowing. EXETER, ST DAVIDS. The station signs became readable as the heavy express eased to a reluc-
tant stop. Brian crooked his neck to peer down the
platform. A brightly coloured magazine kiosk
caught his eye. How had Zoom-man got on against
the seven-headed Zworg? Brian fingered some
loose change in his pocket and glanced across at
Ann. She seemed to be asleep. He peered back towards the kiosk. One or two people were leaving
the train. A man was buying a paper. With another
quick glance towards Ann, Brian eased open the
carriage door and slipped out onto the busy platform. A tinny, west country, voice echoed something incomprehensible over the Tannoy system.

"Quickly, young lady. He's off." The old lady
prodded Ann with a knitting needle. The girl's
eyes flew open. For a moment she felt confused.
Then her eyes took in the open carriage door and
the fact Brian was no longer to be seen. Before you
could blink she was out of her seat and down onto
the platform. She paused, glancing uncertainly
both ways. To the right she sensed rather than saw
a boy rushing off down the platform, and darted
off in pursuit. Reaching the magazine kiosk she
paused again, breathing hard. Her brother was no-
where to be seen. Again she hesitated. Surely it was
another comic he had been after; but there were
quite a few folk jostling around the counter and
he would not have had time to have bought his

Zoom-man and to have returned to the train.

The crowds along the platform were thinning. A porter passed down the train, firmly shutting the carriage doors. Still Ann hesitated, glancing frantically up and down the platform. There was not a Brian to be seen. The guard was raising his flag. Ann hesitated just too long. The train was easing forward, picking up speed. Too late she hurried forward. A porter put out his arm and held her back.

"Careful, miss. Don't get too near."

"B—but—I——" stammered Ann. She felt foolish and helpless. The last coach swayed away towards Cornwall, leaving a bewildered, confused Ann standing staring after it. Now the platform was almost empty, except for the solitary figure of Ann, stranger on a strange station.

CHAPTER TWO

A CRYPTIC CLUE

Brian knew nothing of his sister's distress. At the very moment Ann stood bristling with anxiety on Exeter Station, her brother was safe and sound on the Penzance express, which was accelerating away from her in grand style. He had never reached the magazine kiosk. He was half-way down the platform, dodging neatly round a trolley piled high with parcels, when he spotted the Enemy. The lanky, black figure was striding quickly towards the first-class carriages, a newly purchased paper clutched in his thin fingers.

Brian's mind clicked like a cash register. Why buy a new comic when your old one might be regained? No sooner had his agile mind suggested the idea than his active feet leapt to obey. He darted through the first open carriage door and trod on several startled passengers' feet, before stumbling out into the corridor which ran down that side of the train which stood furthest from the station platform. It was at this moment that Ann had gone blundering by on her unsuccessful pursuit towards the magazine kiosk.

Brian hurried along the corridor, back down the

train until he reached the first-class carriages. He slowed to a saunter along this corridor and peered rather rudely into each carriage as he drifted by. At last he spotted him. At least he spotted his thin legs protruding from beneath a spread-open copy of *The Times* which filled one corner seat of the comfortable compartment. Brian's hesitation was momentary. He lacked his sister's caution. Pulling open the sliding door, he marched straight into battle. The enemy did not bother to look up from his paper. The other two occupants of the first-class compartment were enormously fat gentlemen, who dozed deliciously by the window, and a rather fearsome looking lady, who wore the biggest hat Brian had ever set eyes on, a hat that was grotesquely decorated with exotic fruit.

"This, young man, is a first-class compartment!" Thunder rumbled as the lady raised her eyebrows. The fat sleeper, obviously her husband, stirred uneasily.

Brian came straight to the point. "I bin robbed!" he announced simply, if dramatically. *The Times* newspaper lowered and the thin-rimmed spectacles rose into view.

"No—not you again." The enemy obviously shared Brian's liking for the direct approach. "Clear off or I'll call the guard."

Brian was not to be so easily daunted. "You stole me comic." Again the unvarnished approach. The fruit-encrusted hat stirred with interest.

"The boy claims you have stolen some property of his," put in the voice from beneath the hat. The Enemy offered her a watery stare which seemed to suggest that the information was both inaccurate and unwelcome.

"The boy is mistaken," he sniffed. "The object in question was confiscated, not stolen. Confiscated to prevent him using it to damage property or persons using Her Majesty's railways!" Considering the argument settled, the Enemy vanished back behind his newspaper. But the lady in the hat had only begun. She swelled to her full height.

"This object," she pushed out a bulky hand and pulled down the top of the newspaper, exposing the Enemy's startled features. "It was a comic paper?"

"It was," said the Enemy coldly, his icy stare attempting to freeze all further discussion. Even Brian's confidence waned; but the lady in the hat was ready with her knock-out blow.

"A comic paper could hardly damage either property or persons," she said triumphantly. "I suggest you give the boy back his property and I will say no more about it!" The fat man shuddered in his sleep.

For a moment silence filled the carriage. By now the train was under way and chose at that moment to pass through a short, screaming length of tunnel. The Enemy seemed to wilt. The eyes glazed beneath the thin-rimmed lenses and at last with a small sigh he dug into the seat beside him, produced a now rather tattered copy of *Zoom-man Comic* and tossed it to Brian before retreating quickly behind his newspaper.

Brian caught the welcome bundle with a quick gulp of thanks. He had stood watching this spirited exchange with reverent awe. It was not every day he found a champion for his doubtful causes. The lady in the hat returned his grin with an enormous conspiratorial wink. "Now run along, young man." Her haughty voice belied her friendly actions. "Kindly let us get on with our journey in peace."

Brian was happy to do just that and went skipping back along the rocking corridor towards the carriage where he had left his sister. Of course, she was no longer there, and Brian passed the carriage several times before he recognised their luggage and the old lady, who was still knitting at top speed and in complete peace since Brian's sudden departure on Exeter Station. She sighed faintly as the boy eased back into the compartment.

"Seen me sister?" Brian flopped down by the window and stuck his nose into the comic. He was not really interested in the old lady's reply.

"Not since she went out after you at Exeter," she was saying, but Brian heard nothing. Zoom-man was trapped in the cave of the seven-headed Zworg. there seemed to be no escape. The fate of Zoom-man seemed a million times more important than the fate of a mere sister. And so it was that as the train sped towards Plymouth the old lady was able to knit in continued peace and tranquillity.

As the train eased slowly into North Road Station, Plymouth, Brian glanced up from his comic. With mild interest he contemplated the empty seat which his sister had filled during the journey as far as Exeter. Funny she had not returned. He shrugged and struggled open the window to lean out and peer up and down the platform. He had been sure the announcer said 'Brian Kent'. Impossible! But, no, there it was again. He listened hard.

"Would master Brian Kent please leave the train and report to the Station-masters office."

"Hey, that's me." Brian grinned over his shoulder at the old lady. "They want me." He grabbed up his comic, tore open the door, and was gone. Hurriedly the old lady stumbled to the carriage door.

"Wait, boy—your cases——" she was wheezing; but Brian had already vanished into the swaying crowds.

With a glance at the twin cases snug on the over-head rack, the old lady shrugged, eased herself back into her seat and picked up her knitting. "Don't know what the youth of today are coming to," she was still muttering as the train resumed its journey towards the sand and sunshine promised by the holiday posters.

Meanwhile—as they say in all the best books— back on Exeter station Ann had found a friend in the helpful porter who had prevented her attempting to board the moving train.

"Missed the train, little lady?" he grinned. "Not to worry. Not to worry at all. Be another along in just under the hour. Left your small brother all alone on board? Not to worry. I'll get a message through to Plymouth."

And so it was that with a whole string of messages 'not to worry' buzzing in her head Ann caught the next rain through to Plymouth and caught up with her brother just as he was finishing off his fifth ice-cream under the benevolent eye of a Devonshire railway clerk.

"Fancy you getting lost like that," burst out Brian as his sister came blushing into the station office. "Mum said you're s'posed to look after me. She should have told me to look after you."

Ann was speechless with relief at having found her brother again and said very little until she found out that Brian had left their cases on the train. "Stupid's not the word for you, Brian Kent," she fumed. "What you want to do a brainless thing like that for? How we going to get our clothes and things back?"

The station clerk looked on and grinned at this fond family reunion. "Not to worry, kids," he put in, when the quarrel looked ready to explode. "We'll phone through to Penzance and get your stuff delivered back to Truro. Won't arrive till tomorrow now, though."

The clerk was as good as his word. He rang through about their luggage and then made sure that they were safely installed aboard the last train to leave for Cornwall. "Not far now," he chuckled. "And don't forget to get off at Truro."

As the train passed slowly over Brunel's great bridge which spans the Tamar into Cornwall, Brian pressed his nose flat against the carriage window and peered at the ships far below. Ann picked up his now discarded *Zoom-man Comic* and idly thumbed through the picture strips. She felt much too old to actually bother to read any of this stuff. She turned the comic over. The back page comprised a full-page advert for *Zap-Zonk Comic*, another of Brian's literary delights.

Curious, thought Ann. Someone had been scribbling neat little names and figures. "Hey, Brian," she ventured after a while. "Is this that man's writing?" Brian had explained in graphic and exaggerated detail the story of retrieving his treasure from the tall, thin villain of the piece. Brian turned from his nautical studies and blinked at the comic. "S'pose so," he offered with a shrug. "Tisn't mine."

"But look, the name of the place were going to is on here," she puzzled. "Look." She pointed to the neatly inscribed name, Ferryman's Folly. Alongside was printed the sum, £50,000. There followed a list of other names neither of the children recognised. "You don't think that man has anything to do with Aunt Jocelyn and Uncle Joseph, do you?" sighed Ann. She felt her spirits sinking. "If he has, you may have spoiled our holiday before it's really got under way. Once he tells them about your behaviour on the station and train they'll probably lock us both away somewhere safe for the month!"

Brian peered hard at the name. "Looks like the same name," he said at last with an air of authority. "But I 'spect it's a different place altogether." Brian was the perpetual optimist. "Yes, sure to be somewhere different. Man who gets upset just 'cause he trips over a bit of luggage is *sure* to belong somewhere different to our relations!" he ended triumphantly. He turned his attention back to the panorama of Devonport harbour. In his mind the matter was settled. But Ann was not so easily convinced.

People that Brian annoyed had an unpleasant habit of turning up just where they could do most damage.

The remainder of the journey down through the woods and hills of Cornwall proved uneventful. The children had a compartment to themselves, and not even Brian could raise the hackles of an empty seat, even if his restless fidgeting could dull the edge of the springs. At long last the train was pulling into their destination.

"Truro. Truro. Change here for Falmouth," echoed the Tannoy.

The children scrambled down onto the platform, with Ann fishing in her pocket for the tickets. "No-one here to meet us," she grumbled, as she led her brother out into the road outside. Then she remembered. Of course, their relations would have met an earlier train—the one she had lost at Exeter and Brian had left at Plymouth. The sensible thing would have been to have sent a message through to Truro. Still, too late now. She dug out her purse and peered into it at her hard-saved holiday money. With a sigh she approached a battered taxi which stood parked outside the station.

"Where to, me dears?" smiled the driver.

"Ferryman's Folly—er, Gill Creek, it is."

"Ah—I knows it." The driver swung open the rear door. "Can't take 'ee all the way—but up-a-long a bit of ways."

Not quite knowing where or what 'up-a-long a bit of ways' was, the children still climbed thankfully into the cab.

"No luggage?" grinned the driver, as he slipped

behind the wheel. "Arn't 'ee going t' stay long?" The children said nothing but relaxed as the car sped through the granite grey streets of the Cornish town. A steep climb brought them out into the country. Glancing back over her shoulder, Ann could see the prominent spires of the great cathedral highlighted by the evening sun.

The roads grew narrower, as the overgrown hedges crowded in round the taxi. Twisting and turning, the way led into cool valleys and smooth tunnels of foliage. At last the driver pulled up alongside a small wood. The road was just a narrow lane imprisoned between tall hedges. "Here us be," he announced cheerfully. He leapt out and swung open the rear door. Slightly bemused, the two children got out and stood looking vainly for any sign of a house.

The driver pointed to a wooden stile, which offered access to an overgrown path up through the woods. "Just down-a-long there and 'ee can't miss 'un."

Ann thanked the driver politely as she counted the fare into his horny hand. Brian was already over the stile and ploughing into the undergrowth. Ann followed a little more carefully. In the silence of the evening she could hear the taxi reversing back the way it had come. Blackberry brambles tore at her dress. Twice she was stung by nettles; but still she pressed on after her brother. The path wound carelessly upwards through the woods. After the stuffy train and taxi, the heavily scented evening air was welcome. At the crest of the hill, the trees thinned out and the path skirted a field.

Here Ann paused to get her bearings. From her feet the smooth contours dipped into a rich, green valley of trees. Deep in the heart of this soft covering she glimpsed the silver sheen of a winding river, sleek and mysterious in the dying light of the sun. The waters drew her feet down the little worn path, which plunged again into the trees.

"Quick, Annee. Look at this!" Brian was calling, his voice shrill on the evening air.

Ann caught him up. The path ended at the river, just a tiny, wooden landing-place marking where it vanished into the water.

"What we do now—swim?" asked her brother.

Ann was peering at a faded board, which had been nailed askew to the twisted trunk of a convenient tree.

"Call out for the ferry," she muttered. "That's what it says." She tried to peer across the broad stretch of river, but here the trees bowed their branches low over the water and obscured the view of the far bank.

"What do you call?" puzzled Ann with a shrug of her now tired shoulders.

"Ahoy, of course," put in Brian at once. "Like this: Ahoy, there! Send us a boat." His voice rose clear and shrill.

Now the light was fast fading and the woods seemed dark and mysterious. Brian called again, his voice breaking as he tried to reach across the water.

They waited. A chill wind rustled across the water. A branch creaked ominously. Ann shivered and glanced quickly over her shoulder. Across the water, out of the shadows, moved a dark shape. With strangely muffled creaks it came nearer. Somewhere in the woods behind a stray animal rushed headlong through the undergrowth.

Slowly Ann reached out and took her brother's hand.

CHAPTER THREE

THE ENEMY SIGHTED

"Well, hello there! You must be Ann and Brian."
As the cheery voice rang out across the water all
the mystery and melancholy of the evening
vanished like a forgotten dream and a new atmo-
sphere seemed to clothe the river and woods.

"Better late than never," went on the cheerful
voice, as a cumbersome rowing-boat was skilfully
manoeuvred alongside the wooden landing-place.
An enormous smile of welcome filled their uncle's
large, red face. "Come on now. All aboard."

Ann took the helping hand her uncle was offering and stepped gingerly down into the ferry-boat.
She sat down quickly and held onto the bench seat
as Brian came bounding after her. With a strong
shove, Uncle Joseph worked the boat away from
the overhanging trees and dug his oars into the
flashing water. "Thought you'd missed the train,"
he went on. "Your Aunt Jocelyn was hanging about
Truro station all afternoon. We didn't know what
to do when you failed to show up."

"We did miss the train—sort of," offered Ann.
She was much too tired for full explanations at
present. Now they were clear of the bank, the full

sweep of the river came into view. The fading light showed mysterious wood-clad banks dipping smoothly down to kiss the sparkling silver water. Ann had always associated Cornwall in her mind with craggy cliffs and sun-drenched beaches and little fishing coves rather than with the secluded softness of this peace-filled river.

"This is a branch of the River Fal," explained her uncle, reading the unspoken question in Ann's eyes. "It's more of a valley drowned by the sea than the sort of river you're used to. It's nearly full tide now and you are seeing Gill Creek at its best."

"That where we're going to stay, Uncle?" Brian pointed enthusiastically to the approaching bank. Out of the trees peeped one of the strangest little houses Ann had ever set eyes on. There were weird, pointed towers and oddly shaped windows.

"That's it," smiled Uncle Joseph. "Ferryman's Folly. And for the next month it's all yours."

Aunt Jocelyn came hurrying down to meet them as the two children scrambled ashore. She was smiling, plump and full of cheerfulness. As soon as Ann felt her warm hug of welcome she knew this was going to be the best holiday they had ever enjoyed. Soon they were settled snugly in the perfectly round living-room of the Folly, sipping steaming mugs of cocoa and pouring out the story of their adventurous journey by train. Uncle Joseph came in half-way through. Ann noticed that he walked with a pronounced limp.

"Well, now," bustled Aunt Jocelyn, as she saw Brian's eyelids beginning to droop. "Time for bed. I've given you the tower bedrooms. Did you notice the Folly has two little towers? You'll get a marvellous view of the river from up there and you'll be able to signal to each other and anything you youngsters like getting up to."

Ann was too tired for views or signalling. Sleepily, she followed her aunt up a winding staircase and found herself in a completely round bedroom with plain white walls and the neat little bed set right in the centre of the room.

"Just like sleeping in a lighthouse," she giggled.

"Now I expect you'll want to give thanks for a safe journey," smiled Aunt Jocelyn. Ann flushed. Saying her prayers was the last thing she was thinking of.

"I've left you a little Bible, Ann," went on her aunt, pointing to the bedside table. "I expect you put yours in your lost cases."

Ann shrugged when her aunt had left the room. She had not troubled to bring a Bible. As soon as she had changed into the slightly large, borrowed pyjamas her aunt had found to take the place of her own which were now most probably sitting in a suitcase in Penzance, she sat on the bed and picked up the small white Bible. Ferryman's Folly seemed a fascinating spot and Aunt Jocelyn seemed awfully nice, but she hoped her aunt would not be bringing religion into everything all through the holidays.

The Bible fell open at the Psalms and Ann read a few words. "The lines are fallen unto me in pleasant places; yea, I have a goodly heritage." She was not altogether sure what it meant but it sounded beautiful. Quietly she did kneel. For the

first time for over a year she said her prayers before
slipping between the crisp, cool sheets. As she lay
slipping down into the warm arms of sleep, the
Bible verse drifted smoothly across her mind. "The
lines are fallen unto me in pleasant places." Soon
she was as soundly asleep as her brother Brian in
the tower at the opposite corner of the house.

Morning came early at Ferryman's Folly. In
London, people sleep on through the best hours
of the day, when the sun is fresh born and the air
alive with vitality. The sound of Aunt Jocelyn
raking out the fire in the living-room somewhere
in the house below woke Ann not long after the
birds reached the peak of their morning chorus.
Still half asleep she swung out of bed and yawned
her way across to one of the windows. Jerking back
the brightly coloured curtains, she stared out into
the morning. A low mist curled over the river, and
the trees hung motionless in the damp morning
air. Ann toured each of her four windows and
sampled the view in each direction. Behind the
house the woods rose steeply; in front lay the river,
curving away up and down the valley between
lush, green banks.

A pair of matching curtains in the opposite
tower parted and Brian's still sleepy face peered
out. Ann waved, received the return signal, then
drew the curtains before dressing hurriedly after
a quick swill at the hand wash-basin.

"Early bird," smiled Aunt Jocelyn, as Ann came
backing out of the winding staircase, which began
in the living-room. Almost immediately Brian, his
hair tousled, his jumper pulled on back to front,

came sliding down the opposite stairs. "Breakfast not ready till eight, my dears," went on their aunt.

'Could we go for a little walk—just by the river?" put in Ann.

"Of course you can," smiled their aunt. "But just lend Master Brian here a comb and help him get his jumper on straight."

These two little details took hardly any time at all and they were soon heading for the river. The garden ended in a four-foot cliff of crumbling earth which dropped down to a stony beach. One or two ancient rowing-boats lay decaying quietly on the beach. Steps cut in the low cliff led down to a slippery stone jetty. Here was moored Uncle Joseph's ferry-boat and one or two other little rowing-boats. At the end of the jetty a larger motor-boat lay swinging sluggishly with the tide. Tucked under the cliff alongside the jetty was a decaying boat-shed. From inside came the sound of a familiar hymn sung in a deep baritone voice. Despite the early hour Uncle Joseph was hard at work scraping the bottom of a dingy. He looked up with one of his broad smiles when the children sauntered in.

"Nothing like the river for drawing folk early from their beds," he smiled.

"You're at work early," put in Brian, who usually fought for every last second he could spend snug beneath the blankets.

"The day's half over now," grinned Uncle Joseph. "I've already put in an hour or two's fishing." He pointed to a cluster of shining mackerel hanging near the door. "You two get up really early one of these mornings and I'll take 'ee along."

"In the rowing-boat?" put in Brian.

"No. We take the launch. Spinning for that little lot takes me right out from the safety of the harbour into Falmouth Bay."

"That your job?" asked Ann, hoping she was not sounding too nosey. "Fishing?"

"No—the ferry's my job. Folk who use the footpath through the woods give me a shout and I row them over. Like I did you two last night."

"Why don't they build a bridge?" Brian had a practical turn of mind.

"Not enough folk use the crossing to warrant building a bridge, luckily for me," smiled his uncle. "Years ago this was the main route for country folk going into Truro market. Nowadays only hikers and holidaymakers come this way and need my services. Most people have cars and take the road around the head of the river. They say there's been a ferryman here since the Middle Ages though." He stopped to take a close look at a rough patch on the dingy bottom. "Really I'm retired. Before the last war I used to work for Lord Treloar who owned all this land around the river. His Lordship was mad keen on ocean racing and I used to captain his fastest yacht." A far-away look crept into the big man's eyes. "Then when I had my accident"—he tapped his stiff leg—"Lord Treloar gave me a pension and the ferryman's job. He was a good man to work for and this place suits us down to the ground. Beautiful place to live. The sea on my doorstep. What more could an old sailor wish for?"

"It certainly is a marvellous spot, Uncle,"

breathed Ann, her eyes shining.

"Yes, the Lord's been good to me," said Uncle Joseph seriously, and once again Ann felt that slight embarrassment she had experienced the previous evening when her aunt had mentioned praying.

"Hello. Hello. Is there a ferry there?" The high-pitched shout echoed across the water.

"Here we go, then," smiled Uncle Joseph, as he limped from the boat-shed. "Not often we get customers this time of a morning."

The children stood watching him pull the heavy ferry-boat easily across to the far bank. He vanished into the trees. After a slight pause the distant trees stirred their branches and the ferry-boat came gliding back across the river. As the boat slid nearer, Ann suddenly clutched Brian's arm and drew him hastily back into the shadow of the boat-shed. She had recognised the tall, prim figure in the stern. It was the Enemy.

'What's *he* want?" growled Brian. "After me comic again."

"Told you he was something to do with Ferry-man's Folly," hissed Ann. "Now he'll go and tell them all about your antics yesterday and our holiday will be spoilt." Ann had been careful to play down her brother's escapades when she had told her aunt about the trip down.

The ferry-boat glided smoothly alongside the jetty and Uncle Joseph swung ashore and helped the Enemy to clamber awkwardly after him. To Ann's surprise, her uncle did not seem to know their friend of yesterday. With a curt "Good-morning to you", the Enemy stalked off, his black business-suit looking completely out of place in this relaxed holiday setting. He took the path which skirted the Folly garden and led up through the trees over the next hill. Just before vanishing into the green background the Enemy paused to stare hard and long at Ferryman's Folly.

"Queer sort of hiker all togged up like that," Uncle Joseph was grinning as he came limping back into the shed.

"He's an enemy, that's what he is," muttered Brian darkly.

"Don't be silly," fussed Ann. But the name was to stick and become the name the stranger would keep until the end of the adventure.

"Your uncle has fixed a surprise for you," announced Aunt Jocelyn brightly as the two hungry children finished off an excellent breakfast.

"Sort of surprise," put in their uncle with one of his broad smiles.

"What is it?" Brian hopped off his chair and spun in a circle.

"Ah, now. You have to find it," winked Uncle Joseph. "As soon as you've brushed your teeth, take the path that runs along by the river to the left of the house. Once you've made your way around the point where two arms of the river meet, you can't miss it."

"I'll be slipping into Truro to pick up your cases this morning," put in Aunt Jocelyn.

"Not going to walk all the way, are you?" asked Ann quickly. She had seen no car, not even a road at the Folly.

"Hardly," smiled her aunt. "I just have to nip up the path back over the hill and there's a road. We get the St Mawes bus into Truro from there."

Ann and Brian could hardly wait to get on the trail of the 'surprise'. From somewhere Aunt Jocelyn had managed to produce enough old clothes of the right sizes to fit them both out for a day's exploring. At Ann's surprised look she had mumbled something about jumble sales.

Pulling his borrowed anorak closer round his shoulders, Brian led the way along the path which topped the low cliff and ran towards the first bend in the river. They reached it without incident and from their new vantage point could see where Gill Creek met the main waters of the broad valley of the Fal. Here a second creek dipped back into the wooded hills, and almost on the tip of the promontory by the converging creeks nestled an old boathouse.

"Think the surprise is in here?" Brian was about to go bounding off down onto the beach to find out when Ann put a warning hand on his shoulder. "It's him again."

"The Enemy!" hissed Brian. "What's he doing?"

The Enemy stood tall and thin as ever, attempting to focus a pair of binoculars on to the far bank. The children stood and watched until he lowered the binoculars and moved purposefully away through the trees.

"What's he matter, anyway?" shrugged Brian. He scrambled in a flurry of earth and stones down the low cliff and squelched into the muddy sand. Ann found some easier way to follow and had soon joined her brother at the disused boathouse.

"Nothing in here," grunted Brian, leaping down from the concrete slipway which led up into the unoccupied interior.

"Something up above, though," mused Ann, pointing to the wooden steps which led up to a door in the rear gable-end. The two children climbed the steps. On the door was written in felt-tip pen, SURPRISE! SURPRISE!

"This is it!" shouted Brian. He flung open the door and marched boldly inside.

CHAPTER FOUR

ALIENS HAVE LANDED!

Ann followed her brother through the door into the old boathouse loft. The long, attic-like room ran the full length of the building towards a large window looking out across the sparkling river. Over the window had been hung a crudely cut cardboard notice, which announced in the same felt-pen style they had noticed on the door, HOLIDAY DEN.

Immediately alongside the door a stout wooden table was arranged against the wall. Ann turned to it at once. Over it was pinned another note stating, KITCHEN—*enjoy yourself, Ann!* Half the table was filled by a twin burner camping-gas stove. Under the table squatted a fat little cylinder. Over the stove was yet another note explaining in detail exactly how the thing was to be lit and used. There were also a whole string of warnings about the dangers of fire. Ann smiled. She knew all about using these little stoves. She always did the cooking when the family went camping.

STORE CUPBOARD, announced a tall wooden locker. Ann peeped inside. It was chock-a-block with tinned foods of all sorts. She read the inevitable notice pinned inside the door. *Use whatever you fancy, Ann dear. I'll give you fresh food—you know, eggs and things—to take out every day. You can cook your own mid-day meals in the Den. Thought it would make a change from having to treck back to the Folly every day. Don't forget to be in for an evening meal at seven every night, though. Love, Aunt Jocelyn.*

Ann glowed with pleasure. She had her very own kitchen. She turned to examine the rest of the room.

In the centre stood a table and four chairs, marked DINING-ROOM. In front of the window two deck-chairs had been arranged with a view stretching to the opposite hillside. One carried the label, LOUNGE. But it was the object in front of the chairs that was riveting Brian's attention. It was a shining brass telescope which pivoted from a solidly placed tripod. Already the boy's eye was glued to the eye-piece as he scanned the woods across the river.

FOR KEEPING AN EYE ON PIRATES, read the notice dangling from a loop of string. "Hey, this is really great!" enthused Brian, swinging the telescope in a wide arc. "You can see for miles."

Ann flopped into a deck-chair and stared happily out across the water. Their very own Den. Her heart bubbled with happiness. The early morning mist had long since lifted and now just a few wispy clouds chased across the blue, blue sky. The perfect calm of this secluded spot drew the gentle heat of a flawless July morning. Across the river nothing stirred. The far bank formed a completely wooded slope except for one lighter green patch of grass nestling snug amongst the surrounding trees.

"I can see a house!"

Ann wondered idly why her brother had to shout. She was almost touching his elbow.

"Let's look." Ann straightened up and pulled her brother's collar. Reluctantly the boy surrendered the eye-piece. "Only for a minute," he insisted. "Looking for pirates is a boy's job."

Ann had no intention of looking for pirates. She adjusted the focus and slowly explored the opposite hillside. Trees, trees, and more trees. At last she picked out the house, or rather the chimneys of what was obviously a very large house which lay hidden amongst the trees near the summit of the river bank. Somehow a house seemed strangely out of place in this beautiful spot. The boathouse was just right. Small, old, and quaint. The Folly was just right, with its curious towers and lovely gardens, but the thought of anyone else living around Gill Creek seemed an intrusion on the privacy of nature.

Ann focused the telescope on the distant waters of the Fal. A fat pleasure-steamer thrust up-river towards Truro. She could see it was crowded with trippers in garish holiday attire. The boat made no attempt to move in towards Gill Creek, and Ann was suddenly thankful. She had a momentary vision of the peace of this idyllic backwater being shattered by the roar of high-powered motor-launches; of empty soft-drink cans littering the beach, blaring transistor radios in the woods, broken glass lurking in the trampled grass, and empty crisp bags blowing in the wind. Yes, she was glad the trippers kept well clear of Gill Creek.

"Come on, girl. My turn now." Brian thrust her impatiently aside.

Ann drifted back to the kitchen end of the Den. She found a giant-size box of matches and tried out the camping stove. Everything was in order and soon she was busy making coffee. "You are to keep away from this end, Brian," she called over her shoulder. "This is strictly my province. And no touching these matches." She put the box on top of the locker and hoped they were out of Brian's reach.

"Hey, Annee—aliens have landed!" Ann was just spooning sugar into the steaming cups as her brother's shrill scream echoed down the loft. She ignored him. "Coffee's up." She set the two cups down on the dining table.

"There's thousands of 'em," her brother was calling. "Millions. It's an invasion!"

Ann knew her brother's wild imagination and continued to turn a deaf ear.

"They got all their gear. Going to set up a base camp."

Ann sighed as she settled onto one of the rickety chairs. Only Brian could turn a spot as peaceable as this into an advance base for an invasion from outer space. She sipped her coffee and felt relaxed.

"Ugly brutes, they are," prattled on her brother.

"You're coffee's going cold," said Ann flatly.

"Ugh, coffee!" sniffed Brian. "Eating and drinking—thats all girls ever think of. D'you s'pose Drake thought about coffee when he was playing bowls and saving England and that?" He came mooching back down the loft and stared at the coffee. "Nothing to eat?"

Ann went back to the store cupboard and found a packet of chocolate biscuits. She half opened it on the table. Brian pounced. "Good thing we was here," he spluttered, his mouth full of biscuit. "We can keep 'un eye on 'em all right." He laughed significantly. "Bet they don't know I spotted their landing."

Bemused, Ann stood up and strolled to the window. Her eyebrows rose as she stared across the river. Brian had been telling a tiny bit of truth. She focused the telescope. There were no two-headed monsters to be seen, but the clearing across the river had definitely been invaded. Four small figures scurried hither and thither. "Very English-looking aliens," she called back over her shoulder.

"Ever heard of disguise?" hissed Brian. He took another biscuit.

"They're campers," said Ann at last. "They're putting up tents."

"Establishing base camp," corrected Brian. He tried another biscuit. It tasted the same as all the others—delicious. Brian had a theory that people who make packets of biscuits put good ones in the end you opened and rotten ones later on. It seemed an opportune moment to test this theory.

Ann watched the frantic activities on the far bank and sighed. More children, noisy children, children like Brian, four of them, could just ruin all her dreams for a peaceful month. She frowned. They did seem rather noisy children. She could see them leaping about and laughing as they erected the two white ridge tents. Two boys and two girls, she mused. Wonder if they're friendly?

Brian came to the end of the packets of biscuits and sighed as he turned the wrapper inside out. This one had been perfect all through. Probably put in deliberately just to hush suspicions, he mused darkly.

"You eaten 'em all?" Ann's eyes boggled as she snatched up the empty wrapper.

"Hungry, wasn't I?" he muttered, returning to his post at the telescope. "Got to keep me strength up when I'm watching aliens. What yu gonna cook for dinner?"

The same question was occupying Ann's mind and she returned to the kitchen end of the loft. There was a plastic bowl and a heavy container of water, which Ann could just lift, that served for the washing-up. She was just wondering where it could be replenished when she read the label attached to the container: *Fresh water tap, down the steps, and around to the right.* "Job for Brian," she grunted to herself as she awkwardly poured the water into the bowl.

That first Saturday flew by. Ann opened a tin of corned beef and settled for instant mash, beans, and the cold meat for lunch. That first of many lunches was just about eatable. The standard of Ann's cooking would improve as the holiday unwound. Brian kept a constant eye on the Aliens and offered an excited running commentary on everything new taking place at the little camp across the creek. As the day wore on, the tide retreated leaving the creek bed a valley of shining mud, just a narrow,

winding snake of water in the centre, showing
where a channel had been dredged. But by the time
the children were ready to leave, the restless fingers
of the sea were beginning to fidget close under the
overhanging trees.

Leaving the Den secure under the protection of
the newly oiled padlock they had found hanging
behind the door, Ann and Brian marched home
along the riverside track. The twin towers of the
Folly showed over the trees. The children reached
the garden and were about to hurry up the path
when they saw the Enemy once again. He was
standing with Uncle Joseph in the side porch of
the Folly. Both men looked slightly angry.

"It's no use whatever, you know," the Enemy was
saying in his dogmatic voice. "Nothing you can do
or say will affect the decision."

Ann drew Brian back into the shade of an overgrown shrub. The two men were moving back
down the path towards the jetty. As soon as the
Enemy had boarded the ferry-boat and their uncle
had started to creak away across the water, Ann led
the race to the door.

"Who was that, Auntie?" she burst out, as she
hurried into the dining-room. Aunt Jocelyn looked
on the verge of tears.

"No-one for you to be worrying your head about,
love," she said quickly. "Have a quick wash, both
of you. Food'll be on the table when you come
down." She turned away and busied herself with
arranging knives and forks.

Upstairs in her tower bedroom, Ann peered
down from her window and saw Uncle Joseph

rowing back very slowly across the river. The Enemy had gone. She watched her uncle limp along the jetty and disappear into the boat-shed. He seemed a hundred years older than the happy man they had been speaking to that morning so early.

At the meal table her aunt and uncle were strangely hushed. Brian prattled on about telescopes and aliens but the couple did not seem to be listening. Ann added her thanks for the super den and won a shy smile from their uncle.

"Thought that would be just what you'd need."

"Your uncle got it all ready as soon as we knew you were coming for sure," added Aunt Jocelyn. Their gloom began to lift.

"I've been getting a little dingy ready for you both," mused Uncle Joseph, as Brian tucked into his second helping of afters. "I'll give you a few lessons on the oars and make sure you can handle her first, though."

"Great!" burbled Brian, and Ann's face glowed bright.

After the enormous meal, Aunt Jocelyn set deck-chairs on the terrace and they all sat watching the blood-red sun dip slowly over the distant hills.

"Why *is* the place called a folly?" asked Ann, after a while. Brian had grown tired of just sitting and had scampered off down to the beach to toss stones into the river.

"Built by the late Lord Treloar when he was a young man and lived for his yachts," explained Uncle Joseph, with a nod towards the quaint old house. "He had the old ferryman's cottage pulled down and this one put up in the place. In those days the channel was dredged deeper and there was always an ocean-going yacht or two moored in the river here." His eyes took a dreamy haze. "The old Lord was a bit of a wild young man and the Folly was his idea of a joke. Still, over the years the building has mellowed and now tones in completely. You can't help growing to love the old place." He exchanged a slightly sad look with his wife.

"Did Lord What's-'is-name live here?" put in Ann.

"Lord Treloar? No. He lived in the Big House, over the next creek. Penrye House. You can just see it in the trees from the boathouse."

The chimneys, thought Ann and said out aloud: "Does this Lord still live there?"

"Died six months back." Genuine sorrow misted the old sailor's eyes. "Place is empty now. Up for sale."

"Some boys and girls camping over near it," said Ann.

"So I gathered from your brother's talk of aliens," laughed her uncle. "Folk often camp in that clearing. Good spot. Got to have permission, though."

As Ann settled down to sleep in her round bedroom, she pondered the events of their first day at the Folly. Everything had been perfect except for the unwelcome appearance of the Enemy. What was this thin stranger doing snooping around Gill Creek? What had he said to so upset her aunt and uncle? Who was he? But sleep came long before any satisfying answer to these persistent questions, and once more the gentle hands of darkness wreathed the Cornish night in peace.

CHAPTER FIVE

SUNDAY SURPRISES

Next morning the children were much later in rising, and by the time they came whirling down the spiral staircases breakfast was ready.

"Got the boat ready, me dear," said Uncle Joseph cheerfully, as he strode into the room just as Ann was finishing off her third piece of toast.

"Going for a trip, are we?" Brian's eager eyes flashed.

"We are. And in our best clothes," smiled Aunt Jocelyn.

"Best clothes?" echoed Brian.

"Yes. Got your cases from the station yesterday," went on his aunt. "You'll find your suit hanging in the wardrobe, and I see Ann has brought some pretty dresses along."

"But where we going, in our best clothes, in a boat?" puzzled Ann.

"To church—where else on a Sunday?" laughed Uncle Joseph.

"Church!" sniffed Ann, half to herself. Still, the boat trip sounded nice and she did want to try on one of the new print dresses her mum had bought for the holidays.

Back up in her room she tried on the yellow dress with the broad belt. She did not like it and tried on the blue with the full skirt. She whirled in the centre of the room in front of the dressing-table mirror. It would do. Her hair was a bit of a mess. It took ten minutes brushing to get it flowing smoothly over her shoulders as she liked it. By then her aunt was calling up the stairs.

"Hurry up, Ann—and you, Brian. Mustn't be late."

By the time Ann swept down into the living-room, Brian was a boy transformed. His new blue suit was sharp pressed, his hair sleek and combed. He looked indignant.

"Right. Off we go." Aunt Jocelyn fussed them both down the garden to the waiting motor-launch. Clean, bright cushions lay scattered across the seats. With great dignity Ann seated herself along a side seat. Brian almost plunged into the river but his uncle's strong grip saved the day. Soon the neat white launch was softly chugging past the tree-clad banks down-river.

They rounded the promontory where the old boathouse kept its lonely watch out across the river. Ann could just see the two small tents high in the woods. There was no sign of the four aliens. By now the launch was pushing against the tide up the creek which angled off from Gill Creek.

"Ruan Creek, this," said Uncle Joseph, who seemed to have an uncanny knack of anticipating Ann's unspoken questions. "Leads up to Ruan Village. This is the best way for us to get to church of a Sunday—by river. Could walk but it's a long way round and murder on the feet."

Suddenly he reached out, switched off the engine and let the launch glide silently through the swishing water. "Look," he pointed, his voice falling to a whisper. The two children followed his directing finger. Close under the shore a heron stood poised in the shallows. The launch slipped lazily towards him, at last sending him flapping noisily away up-river. Uncle Joseph grinned and restarted the engine which was boxed amidships.

"Peace and quiet," he muttered, "that's what wild life needs."

"They certainly get plenty of that around here," breathed Ann, gazing out across the silky smoothness of the creek.

"They do at the moment," agreed her uncle, a little grimly. "Let's hope it stays that way."

Something in his tone made Ann glance quickly in his direction, but the placid round face offered no clues as to what anxieties were disturbing or threatening to disturb the retired yachtsman. Now they were rounding the next bend and beginning to nose towards a cluster of cottages which formed Ruan Village. Uncle Joseph brought the vessel gently alongside the tiny jetty where one or two other boats bobbed and curtsied in the ebbing tide.

Their destination was a small, granite chapel which huddled between the white-washed cottages, half-way up the steep village street. A friendly man at the door offered them hymn-books and a smiling welcome. Soon they were squeezing into the worn pews half-way down the plain little building. The hymns were well-known and mostly by Charles Wesley. Ann enjoyed the singing, even though the shrill voice of Brian kept wandering off into some private tune of its own. The minister seemed a kindly old man with a pleasant face and soft white hair. His sermon was easy to follow and Ann found herself thoroughly enjoying the all-too-short service.

The children's aunt and uncle seemed well-known at the village church, and they found themselves being introduced to a bewildering variety of friendly Cornish folk. They found that they would not be returning to the Folly till evening. Uncle Joseph pointed down towards the jetty and Ann saw that the retreating tide had left the launch high and dry on the mud.

They shared Sunday lunch with the minister and his wife at the little rose-covered cottage at the top of the hill. The meal was simple but splendid. Ann joined the minister's wife in the tiny scullery to help with the washing-up. The minister's wife was a plump, motherly soul.

"What a beautiful place," sighed Ann, gazing out of the window and down across the river.

"The Lord is good to us, my dear," smiled the woman simply.

Ann flushed. It was the second time she had heard this expression used. "God seems real when Auntie and Uncle talk about Him," she said hesitantly.

"He is real, my dear," smiled the minister's wife. "Do you think all that beauty got there by accident?"

That afternoon Ann thought a lot about those words. The two children were on a walk across the hill, with Brian dashing off ahead and tearing through the undergrowth and swinging from passing branches. At school the teachers seemed to say that the whole world had sprung into being by accident. Ann found it hard to believe. She found it even harder to believe as she topped a rise and stood looking out over the rolling beauty of the Cornish landscape, with the silver serpent of the Fal shining in the middle distance. There must be a God, she found herself thinking. A God who is powerful and good.

"God must love people an awful lot to give them such a marvellous world to live in," she found herself bursting out to her uncle when they at last got back from the walk.

"He does," smiled her uncle. "The world is only ugly where men have made it ugly."

The evening service in the little church proved even more interesting than the morning. The speaker was a tall young man who had motored over from Truro for the occasion.

"He's a missionary," Aunt Jocelyn whispered to Ann, as he rose to speak.

Soon he had even Brian enthralled as he told of his adventures in the forests of South America. Apparently he had spent the last five years attempting to get friendly with just one particularly wild tribe of Amazon natives. Slowly he had struggled to learn their language and had just begun to teach them to read and write. His great ambition was to return with the Bible translated into their language. It made Ann feel a little guilty to think she had a Bible at home and never read it.

"The rich beauty of those tropical jungles has to be seen to be believed," said the young missionary, his firm voice ringing out round the crowded building. "If only the lives of men and women could be restored to that perfect beauty we lost through sin! But we believe in the power of God's grace to transform the lives of those who receive Christ."

As the launch purred back down the creek, Ann sat with one hand trailing in the water, her thoughts full of the missionary's words. Grace sounded like something very wonderful if it could change the way people behaved. She decided to ask her aunt to explain about it when they got home. As they approached the old boathouse they heard a wild chanting and noticed a yellow flicker of light dancing out across the evening waters. Ann peered ahead.

On the shore right opposite their den a fire of driftwood blazed and crackled in the slight breeze. Round and round the blaze, wearing only bathing costumes, their faces blackened, danced and pranced four weird figures.

"Must be them campers," mused Ann.

"Hope they'll be careful with that fire." Uncle Joseph edged the launch nearer. The chanting was wild and punctuated with giggles.

"A savage Amazon tribe," breathed Brian, his mind still filled with the missionary's stories. The Aliens paused, breathless, as they saw the launch slipping by.

"Ola Ola, ugh!" shouted the biggest boy, brandishing a wooden spear in their direction. The smallest boy leapt up and down and banged his chest in a gorilla-like manner.

"Unfriendly natives!" laughed Uncle Joseph. "Obviously we would not be welcome at their beach party."

The two girls on the beach did not join in the boy's antics. They stood slightly embarrassed and just watched the launch chug by.

"Heathens!" breathed Brian. "In need of some fearless missionary to penetrate their jungle home. Don't even know English, they don't. Wonder if there's any Bibles in their language. Ola. Ola Ugh." He repeated the words over and over to himself. "Don't seem to recollect that language. It's not French."

The launch was now swinging round to enter Gill Creek. Ann glanced back. The Aliens were now squatting round the fire. They seemed to be trying to extract potatoes from the heat with small pieces of stick. She glanced at the boathouse with its strip of shelving beach. Plans glowed in her head. They, too, would have a fire and cook out of doors. If only they had tents! she found herself wishing. Of course, the towers rooms were marvellous. But *tents*. Little tents. Not like the cottage-like frame tent they shared with their parents on camping holidays. *Real tents*. There was a fine strip of grass just a little way from the old boat-house. If only . . .

CHAPTER SIX

ALIENS, AHOY!

"Tents!" announced Uncle Joseph next morning as the children sat down to breakfast. He came striding into the dining-room and dumped two dusty-looking duffle bags onto the floor. "One each," he went on. "Neatest little pair of ridge tents you'll set eyes on. Dug them out of the attic."

Ann's eyes boggled. How was it that her uncle could guess her thoughts?

"Joseph! Not on the clean carpet," fussed Aunt Jocelyn, sweeping into the room with a jug of hot milk. "You ought to have more sense."

"Sorry, dear," he apologised, with a wink at Brian. "I'll unpack them on the lawn. Just to make sure they are habitable. Could you dig out a pair of sleeping-bags from under the stairs?"

"We going to *sleep* in 'em?" enthused Brian, bounding off his chair and forgetting all about his breakfast.

"If you eat your breakfast, we'll see," smiled Aunt Jocelyn, catching him by the collar and returning him to his seat at the table.

Never had breakfast sped by more quickly. Brian even went without his customary fourth

ALIENS, AHOY! 55

piece of toast. Outside on the lawn in the morning
sunshine, Uncle Joseph had unpacked both smart
green tents and was examining them carefully for
signs of rot and wear.

"As good as new," he announced, just as Aunt
Jocelyn came hurrying out with two gaily coloured
sleeping-bags. "There's a fair site just at the back
of the boathouse."

"Know just where you mean," said Ann at once.
She had already planned in her mind the exact
setting for their adventure camp.

"Think you can get these things set up?" Uncle
Joseph was carefully repacking the tents.

"Dead simple," cut in Brian. "If Ann don't
know, I'll give 'er a 'and."

Ann had to smile. "Grab your tent then, super-
boy," she laughed. "Let's see how good you are at
humping."

"I'll get Uncle Joseph to bring the sleeping-bags
round after I've aired them," called their aunt
after the fast-retreating figures. "You can only
sleep out if you promise to be good and there's no
threat of rain about."

"Rain," snorted Brian, from beneath his weighty
bundle. "It never rains on holidays."

By the time Uncle Joseph came chugging round
in the launch with the aired sleeping-bags and a
couple of pillows and groundsheets, the neat green
tents stood proudly in the sheltered clearing just a
stone's throw from the boathouse. Brian had
struggled hopelessly with his tent while Ann
erected hers single-handed. "Mine's more difficult
than yours was," he pouted as his sister came across

to get him out of his tangle of guy ropes and sagging poles.

"Come back to the boathouse," smiled their uncle after he had finished admiring the camp. "Another little surprise."

Brian raced ahead, stumbling and panting, in the excitement of yet another surprise. "The dingy!" he cried as he spotted the smart little rowing-boat bobbing behind the launch. "You've brought it."

"Her," corrected Uncle Joseph, grasping the painter and drawing the little vessel in-shore. "Meet the *Lady Peregrine*."

"She's beautiful," enthused Ann, recognising the dingy her uncle had been working on the previous Saturday.

"Super!" echoed Brian.

"Not a bad little job," summed up their uncle with a smile. "But can 'ee handle her?"

" 'Course we can!" broke in Brian; but Ann shrugged doubtfully.

"We shall see," grinned Uncle Joseph.

And see he did. Perhaps it would be better to pass over this particular afternoon in silence in order to spare Ann's blushes and Brian's pride. All that is needed to be said is that the afternoon proved full of incident as the two children attempted to master the rudiments of handling a pair of oars and a rather stubborn-minded *Lady Peregrine*. To gloat over the number of times Brian had to be towed off a mud bank, and to dwell on the number of times Ann's oars missed the water and she ended up in the bottom of the boat with her legs flapping in the air, would be to detract something from the hero image you may have been building up around our two young friends. Suffice it to say that by the end of the afternoon both children had gained a glimmer of nautical sense.

"Don't forget," warned Uncle Joseph as he helped them drag the dingy up the slipway past the high-tide mark. "Always wear those life-jackets when you're afloat. I know you can both swim—after a fashion—but if I catch either of you afloat without a life-jacket, this dingy comes home to Ferryman's Folly."

The evening was clear and warm, with not a sign of rain. They stood waving goodbye to their uncle's launch, still flushed with the triumphant thought that they would be spending their first night alone under canvas.

"Bit of a nuisance these things, but awful sensible," said Ann, as she unfastened her yellow life-jacket and tossed it into her tent. She fingered the whistle her uncle had left. "A couple of sharp blasts and I'll come running," he had promised with a grin. "But don't get me out of bed for the first stray fox that comes sniffing round in the night."

As the light faded, Ann built a driftwood fire just along from the boathouse and the two children sat side by side on a groundsheet, knees drawn up to their chins, listening to the wind rippling across the water and stirring the surrounding trees. After a while, lights flickered on the distant shore. The sound of shouts drifted across the creek. Ann felt suddenly lonely. The Aliens were building another beach fire.

"Can't we go over and join 'em?" Brian put Ann's secret thoughts into words. "Could easily do it in the dingy."

"We mustn't," said Ann doubtfully. "Not in the dark."

"It's not dark," replied Brian at once, his eyes pleading up into his sister's face. "Not *really* dark."

Ann said nothing. She sat wrestling with temptation in silence. Across the river came a happy chanting which dissolved into squeals and giggles. The Aliens were obviously having a great time with their beach fire.

"We oughter go and try 'un teach 'em English," muttered Brian. "Stands to reason everyone oughter know English!"

Ann ignored him. It *would* be fun to get to know the children across the river. The girls seemed nice —well, looked nice—from a distance, that is.

"Come on, then, why not?" Ann sprang happily to her feet.

"Great!" squealed Brian. He was already halfway to the *Lady Peregrine*.

"Wait! Back for your duffel coat and your lifejacket," she commanded. She was carefully extinguishing the beach fire by covering it completely with sand. Her uncle's lecture on fire prevention was being remembered down to the last detail. Reluctantly Brian came back; but soon the intrepid pair, enveloped in cumbersome duffel coats, were shoving the dingy down the slipway and putting to sea. Ann took the oars. So far Brian's oarsmanship left everything to be desired and his sister dare not allow him to take charge, especially on anything as daring and dangerous as a night voyage to an alien shore.

In the trees the shadowy figure of Uncle Joseph at first stirred uneasily; then a smile spread over his broad face. Ann was a sensible girl and it would do them no harm to get to know the campers across the river. Noting with satisfaction that the beach fire was completely dead, he turned his back on the creek and strolled slowly back to Ferryman's Folly.

Ann's arms were still aching from the afternoon's exertions but she pulled steadily at the oars and swung well wide of the promontory where she knew the mud banks lurked. The tide was still full and the river deep. Brian knelt in the bow peering through the dusk, ready to sing out if any obstacle showed. Ann still found it difficult to navigate when she was facing in the wrong direction.

"Left a bit," called back Brian.

"Port," corrected Ann, easing off for a moment on her starboard oar.

"That's what I said," muttered Brian. "Now right a bit."

"Starboard," grunted Ann, but her brother failed to hear.

The Aliens' fire drew nearer as the dingy slipped across the silky surface.

"No-one there," puzzled Brian. Ann twisted to look. The fire still flickered dimly but the beach seemed deserted. Ominously deserted. The bow of the *Lady Peregrine* crunched lightly on the pebbles. Brian leapt ashore, the painter clutched in

his hand. Ann shipped her oars and scrambled
after him. Together they hauled the dingy half out
of the water, and Brian made her fast to a tree-
trunk.

"They've gone," puzzled Ann, as she stood staring down at the flickering fire. "And left their fire
alight. Dangerous, that is." She stooped and
scooped sand over the embers until the last glow
died.

"Let's explore a bit," offered Brian. "We could
make our way inland to their village."

"Village?" echoed Ann.

"Tents," snorted Brian, who had little patience
to spare for sisters who lacked imagination. He was
already moving off up into the trees, tripping and
stumbling in the darkness. Should have brought
electric torches, thought Ann, as she hurried to
keep his shadowy figure in sight. In the best adventure books the heroes all carried electric torches,
even though those torches seemed to share a nasty
habit of running out of battery power just as the
darkest point in the secret passage was reached.
But this was real life and neither of the bold
explorers had remembered to bring those funda-
mental items of the standard hero's kit.

"Sure you're going the right way?" called Ann.
The route ran upwards, steep and unpleasant,
through nettles and brambles galore.

" 'Course!" came her brother's confident reply.
"I know exactly where them tents is."

Ann felt less sure, but suddenly, to her surprise
and Brian's glee, they burst out of the trees and

onto the edge of the clearing so plainly visible from the far side of the river.

"See!" hissed Brian, doing a little jig.

"Sssh," cautioned Ann. They were nearing the pair of white tents, which were somewhat bigger than the Kents'. Double size, thought Ann.

On tip-toe they approached the Alien's camp site. Nothing stirred. Deserted. "Not here, either," ventured Ann, not daring to raise her voice above a stage whisper.

"See that, can't I." Brian sounded annoyed.

"Might as well return to the boat." Ann held out her hands in a gesture of defeat.

"Might as well." Brian's tone shared her feelings.

Slightly dispirited, they drifted back down the hill towards the trees. Soon they were again struggling through the shadowy wood.

"Must have heard us coming for miles," grunted Ann, as she barked her shins for the umpteenth time that night.

"Should'a brought torches," muttered Brian. Now *he* was reading her thoughts.

At last they dropped down onto the pebbly beach.

"Let's get the dingy and go home," yawned Ann. She peered up and down in the semi-darkness. There was no sign of the *Lady Peregrine*. "Must have strayed off course in the trees," she muttered. "Look along the beach a bit, Brian." They trudged to the right. Not a boat to be seen.

"Must have been the other way." Ann bit her

lip anxiously. They trudged back to the left. Still no sign of the *Lady Peregrine*.

"She must have drifted off down the river." Brian put his sister's unspoken fears into words.

"Don't be silly. We dragged her ever so far up the beach and you tied the painter to a tree. You *did* tie her securely, didn't you?"

" 'Course I did," muttered Brian crossly. "Saw me, didn't you?"

Ann fingered the whistle her uncle had given her, in her duffel coat pocket. Would her uncle hear it across the water? The night was quiet and she had read somewhere about sound carrying for miles across water. She decided he *would* hear the whistle for help. But dare she use it? If their uncle found them stranded on the far side of the creek, the dingy drifted who knows where, surely he would never trust them again to sleep out in tents? At last she sighed, "We'll have another look." Without much hope they trudged back along the shore.

"This is where the fire was," said Ann, pausing to prod the sand with a stick.

"An' here's the tree I tied the boat to," indicated Brian. They stood glumly staring out across the empty waters. The *Lady Peregrine* had vanished without trace.

"Hi there! Is that you, Master Tom?" The sudden voice made them both jump. It was a harsh voice they both immediately recognised. A powerful flashlight beam stabbed the shadows. Ann blinked in the overpowering light. The beam shifted to Brian. "Not *you* again!" barked the voice. Brian cringed, backed away. Ann tried to peer into the trees where the voice originated. The long, shadowy figure she knew at once.

It was the Enemy!

CHAPTER SEVEN

NO BETTER THAN HEATHENS!

No one could accuse Brian of thinking slowly. He had a well practised plan for occasions like this. Without further ado and without waiting for the Enemy to say more, he turned and bolted. Off down the beach he galloped, to be swallowed up almost immediately by the murky night. Ann hesitated, gulped, and decided that her brother's plan seemed at that moment an excellent example to be followed without further debate. Before the Enemy could swing his flashlight back in her direction she was off after Brian, her duffel coat flapping wildly. As she ran the Enemy's shout followed her, but she had neither the time nor the inclination to make out the actual words.

She ran till her side ached and she was gulping and gasping for breath. She almost fell over Brian, who had flopped down exhausted on the slightly damp beach.

"Get up," she fussed between great gulps of air. "Catch your death of cold, you will."

Brian pulled himself to his feet and grasped a tree-trunk which at this point grew out across the narrow beach. As their breathing returned to nor-

mal they stood still and listened. There were no
sounds of pursuit to disturb the rustle of the river.
Obviously the Enemy had not felt inclined to give
chase.

"What we do now?" Brian's white features
peered up at his sister. Ann shrugged, stuck her
hands deep into her pockets and again fingered
her uncle's whistle. But if she used it now it might
bring the Enemy crashing through the trees long
before her uncle reached them. What *was* the
Enemy doing lurking in these woods so late at
night. Mystery after mystery seemed to surround
this strange figure. He was always popping up in
some unexpected spot. Who was it that he had
called for? she mused. Master Tom? Could that be
one of the Aliens? Had the Enemy something to do
with the campers from the white tents?

Their flight had taken them some little distance
down the creek but they could still see the distant
shape of the old boathouse. Just behind lay the
green tents, safety, and sleep. Ann yawned deep and
long. A ghostly white moon drifted from a haze of
cloud just above the opposite hillside. It seemed
to hang by magic in the velvet sky. The river shim-
mered in the new soft light.

Was that a boat? Ann's eyes widened. A grey
shape detached itself from the outline of the distant
boathouse and crept across the sparkling water.

"Look, a boat!" Brian had seen it, too.

"The *Lady Peregrine*?" Ann's reply was a mere
whisper.

"It's them Aliens, I bet," muttered her brother.
"Bin over to our camp. What they bin up to over

there?"

"Must have seen us rowing over here," said Ann, indignation growing in her tone. "They hid in the trees and stole our boat when we went up to find their camp!" She felt furious.

Cautiously, they began to make their way back along the beach, one eye on the steadily approaching dingy, one peeled for the Enemy. The *Lady Peregrine* seemed low in the water and crowded. All four Aliens were aboard. The two rather trepid invaders of this alien shore reached the spot the *Lady Peregrine* was heading for, without bumping into sight or sound of the Enemy. They slipped back into the trees and crouched, watching the dingy approach. The largest Alien boy was at the oars. He was handling the craft with expert ease. Their voices drifted ashore.

"Needn't have done that," came a girl's voice. "Bit spiteful, that was."

"Asked for it." A boy's voice. "Who they think they are, busting in on our fire!"

The bow of the *Lady Peregrine* nosed up onto the beach. The smallest boy had leapt neatly onto the pebbles and was securing the painter to an overhanging branch. The two girls came next; the biggest boy at the oars was last to leave.

"They've put our fire out," grumbled the smallest boy, stirring the pebbles with his foot. "What shall we do with the boat? Set her adrift?"

"You'd better not." It was one of the girls. "That would be really spiteful."

"Hey!" said the smallest boy suddenly. "What if them kids are up messing about with our camp?"

"They better not be!" The biggest boy's voice had a stern ring to it. "Come on."

Ann and Brian crouched lower as the four Aliens scrambled up the low cliff and blundered away through the trees.

"Now's our chance," Ann hissed as the sounds vanished into the distance.

Down onto the narrow beach they slid and into the *Lady Peregrine*. Brian loosened the painter, Ann slipped the oars into the rowlocks, and then Brian pushed off and came clambering over the gunwhale as the dingy thrust out onto the moonlit river. They could hardly wait to see what damage the alien landing-party had done to their camp. Hauling the dingy as far as possible up the old slipway into the boathouse, they secured her to a rusty iron ring before dashing round to the camp. Just as Ann had expected, the green tents lay flattened in the moonlight.

"We should'a done it to theirs," snapped Brian.

Ann was too crestfallen and tired to make any comment. She just sighed and set to work to re-erect their canvas sleeping-places. It was an extremely thankful girl who at long last zipped herself into a sleeping-bag and closed weary eyes on a long and eventful day of mystery and excitement.

Next morning the children slept long into the daylight. The sun was already bright with the promise of a blazing July day, when Ann pushed her tousled head out of the tent flaps and saw Uncle Joseph approaching with eggs, bacon, and milk for breakfast.

"What's happened to our early risers?" he

laughed. "Not out late on the river, I hope." His eyes twinked as he noted Ann's blush.

" 'Lo, Uncle!" Brian came bounding and leaping out of his tent. "Going to take us fishing?"

"You are four hours too late for fishing, young man. It's the early worm that catches the fish in these parts."

"When, then?" insisted Brian. "When can we go out with you after fish?"

"How about tomorrow? Can you be ready at five?"

"About tea-time," put in Ann.

"Five in the morning, lazybones," grinned her uncle. "Be ready on the boathouse slipway and I'll pick you up as I go out. If you're not there——" He shrugged his broad shoulders. "I always slip into Falmouth of a Wednesday to get your aunt's grocery order made up. You can come in after we've made our catch and buy any odds and ends you may need."

"Shopping by boat!" breathed Ann. "Marvellous."

Since they would have to rise so early the next morning, the children decided on a fairly peaceful day. While the tide was full they swam for a while in the clear, salt water and then took a turn up the river in the dingy, making a point of keeping well away from the Aliens' shore. When the tide receded leaving a river of mud steaming in the wealth of sunshine, they retreated up into the Den above the boathouse. Here Brian fiddled with the telescope while Ann tried the rather disastrous experiment of cooking peas, potatoes, corned beef, and tinned tomatoes all in the same saucepan. The resulting conglomeration of goo not even the ever hungry Brian would attempt to sample. Finally Ann opened a box of cheeses and they settled for sandwiches.

"Them Aliens are still at it," murmured Brian. The washing-up had been finished and Ann lay back in a deck-chair, leaving Brian still glued to the telescope.

"At it?" Ann closed her eyes and pretended to be asleep.

"Larking about up by their tent. Nasty, spiteful lot."

"The girls didn't seem so bad," put in Ann, always quick to defend her own kind against male attack.

"Can never tell with girls," said Brian darkly.

"Wish we could have been friends with them, though," sighed Ann. She found that the company of just Brian alone was always too much of a good thing.

"That missionary fellow said he took five years to get friends with them natives out by the Amazon. Them Aliens are worst than heathens! Why, I bet them Amazon heathens don't go round knocking people's tents down and stealing their boats and that. Real heathens is civilised. Just like you an' me."

Ann sighed. Brian had a point. The Aliens did not seem the friendliest of children. Still, they had a month to get friendly. That is, if the Aliens stayed that long.

"Missionaries is what them Aliens need," went

on Brian. "Someone oughter row over and make Christians out of 'em. 'Spect I could do it if I had the time."

"Do you really know what a Christian is?" smiled Ann softly. It was a question she had been thinking a lot about, especially since having a little chat with her aunt after church on Sunday.

"'Course I do!" Brian turned and faced his sister. "A Christian is 'n English person who goes to church and that . . ."

"There's more to it than that," corrected Ann. "Didn't you listen to what that missionary said on Sunday? He explained that a real Christian is someone who knows Jesus Christ died for them and has asked for their sins to be forgiven———"

"Well, yes I 'spect there's all that as well," cut in Brian vaguely. He turned back to his telescope as Ann went on: "A real Christian is a person who has asked the Lord Jesus to become the most important person in his or her life." But Brian was no longer listening.

"In fact, I'm not a real Christian." Ann said the words out loud. They startled her, but she knew they were true. The thought had been lurking in her mind ever since the Sunday evening service in the little granite chapel. Of course, Ann went to Sunday school and even to church sometimes, but becoming a real Christian was something more— something more personal.

"Yep," Brian was burbling. "Me and you could be missionaries and go over and convert them Aliens."

"How could we convert them when we need

converting ourselves?" murmured Ann. She rose and thoughtfully left the Den. She wanted to be on her own to think.

"Jolly dangerous," prattled on Brian. "I 'spect we'd have to start converting 'em by just rowing nearby and throwing Bibles and hymn-books and things at 'em. Good thing they aint' got no boat of their own."

And so the day fled by to be replaced by another moonlit evening. But tonight the children did not bother with a beach fire and went off to bed early with an alarm-clock set for four-thirty tucked under Ann's pillow. It proved a fresh, misty morning when the harsh, cheerless rattle of the alarm dragged them both from their sleeping-bags. A quick cup of coffee served for breakfast at this un-heard of hour, and by the time Uncle Joseph's launch came chugging round the promontory they stood duffel-coated and ready on the slipway.

Both children crouched high in the bow as the sleek launch thrust out from the creek into the broad main stream of the Fal. The river lay fresh and deserted at their feet, the birds on both wooded banks filling the morning with golden music.

"Must have been like this on the morning of creation," said Uncle Joseph as he came forward to make a slight adjustment to the engine. The launch was steered by a simple tiller in the stern.

"Can I drive?" Brian came leaping back along the boat.

"Just keep her straight," smiled his uncle, sur-rendering the tiller into an eager, youthful hand. But the boy soon grew tired of the straight course

and tried a little weaving. Uncle Joseph quickly
relieved him of the tiller and sent him grinning
back into the bows. Soon they were moving purposefully out into the broad expanse of the Carrick
Roads, the great heart of Falmouth's magnificent
harbour, where the world's largest ships could have
anchored. Still the launch cut through the waves,
out through the harbour entrance, under the
smiling shadow of Pendennis Castle, which had
been built by Henry the Eighth to keep the harbour free of French pirates. Out in the bay, just off
the whitewashed walls of St Anthony lighthouse,
the waves became sizable and the launch wallowed
and rolled in fine style. Here Uncle Joseph set out
the lines for mackerel fishing. Ann was surprised to
find that no bait was used.

"These bright little spinners snare them,"
smiled her uncle, showing her the tiny metal pro-
pellers with their nasty little hooks.

"You'll never catch nothing, not without bait—
worms or some such thing," pronounced Brian,
with the expert air of the veteran of more than
twenty tiddler-fishing expeditions. But he was to
stare open-mouthed as mackerel after mackerel
came flashing out of the sea, their greedy little
mouths trapped by the clever hooks. After only
half an hour or so cruising up and down between
the waves, they had a fine catch and Uncle Joseph
hauled back in all the lines and stowed them neatly
away till next time.

The launch nosed back into the harbour. Close
under the sides of the deep-sea oil-tankers which
lay under repair in the dockyard, chugged the

children. The great, iron ships made them feel small and insignificant. Then they were cutting through the forest of yachts which lay moored close under the eye of the town itself. Falmouth was a fine sight in the morning sunshine. Terrace upon terrace of quaint, grey houses rose up from the waterside, windows sparkling out across the green slopes of Trefusis just across the placid water.

Uncle Joseph avoided the town pier, with its rows of gaudy pleasure-boats, and landed at the little granite Fish Strand with its narrow Cornish 'op-way' leading up to the twisting main street.

"I'm off to meet a friend—at the bottom of Jacob's Ladder," smiled their uncle. "You enjoy the shops. Meet me back here in an hour."

The children wandered down the cramped streets with its inevitable Woolworths and Marks and Spencers.

"Must send Mum and Dad a card," mused Ann. She selected a harbour view from a newsagents and they set out to discover the post office. It stood waiting for them in the broad valley of the Moor, a great open space in the heart of the town, with steep cliff sides and houses perched clinging up towards the sky, wherever some ledge offered sanctuary. They had posted the card and were strolling across towards the impressive frontage of the Methodist church when they noticed the narrow length of steps climbing away up towards the clouds.

"Think it goes right up to heaven?" asked Brian. A smooth rail followed the course of the big steps. "Be heaven to run up and slide down *that*."

"It's *him* again," gasped Ann suddenly. "He keeps popping up like a jack-in-the-box!"

Sure enough, there at the bottom of the steps stood the enemy, just glancing at his watch. Ann drew her brother back into a shop doorway. Their uncle was approaching. A frown on his face, Uncle Joseph strode up to the Enemy, who offered him a false smile. They muttered for a little while, then moved away together back towards the main street and the harbour.

"Well now," mused Ann. "What do you think of that?"

But Brian was not in a mood for questions. He was already off in hot pursuit, slipping from doorway to doorway in fond impersonation of a trailing detective.

CHAPTER EIGHT

THE FOLLY'S FATE

Through the jostling crowds of holidaymakers pushed the Enemy and Uncle Joseph, with Ann and Brian dodging along in their tracks. Down the busy little street they hurried until at last the children were forced to pull up short. Their quarries had vanished into a black doorway between two shops. Ann stood reading the highly polished brass plate :

'Friendly, Friendly, Friendly and Bott. Solicitors.'

The children hesitated, not quite sure what to do next.

"Wonder what Uncle's doing in there with 'im," muttered Brian.

Ann was wondering exactly the same thing, but she just said, "It's nosey and rude to pry into other folks' business. If Uncle wanted us to know anything about it, he'd tell us."

But Brian was not listening. He was staring at the formidable looking lady who was striding towards them down the street. She wore an enormous, gaily coloured holiday hat. Where had he seen her before? Then he remembered. The hat was different but the same determined light shone in those advancing eyes. It was the woman in the hat from the train. Without glancing down at the small boy who was taking such a pronounced interest in her, the lady in the hat swung open the solicitors' door and disappeared from sight. The door clicked shut.

"What's *she* want in there?" Brian's eyes shone with questions. "I didn't think she was a friend of the Enemy?"

"Don't know her, do we?" Ann turned away from the closed door and began strolling back towards the Fish Strand and the waiting launch. Brian came bounding after her and began to blurt out exactly where he had seen the lady in the hat before.

Ann shrugged her shoulders, as she stood on the quay staring out across the crowded harbour. Pleasure-boats packed with holiday trippers wound in and out of the moored yachts. Across the harbour a gun cracked loudly and a stream of yachts broke line and began to heel and glide out towards the open waters of the Carrick Roads. A race was under way.

Ann shrugged again. The Enemy was still surrounded by mystery.

"They're coming," said Brian after a while. Ann turned. Sure enough, Uncle Joseph, the Enemy, and the lady in the hat were approaching down the slight slope to the quay. They stood for a moment in earnest discussion, then the lady in the hat moved away and Uncle Joseph and the Enemy came on without her. She strode over towards a seat where a portly gentleman snoozed in the sunshine. Ann saw her prod him into wakefulness. He leapt to his feet and waddled off in the wake of his dominant wife.

"Waiting long, kids?" greeted Uncle Joseph. His arms were filled with a giant, cardboard box spilling over with groceries. "Meet my niece and nephew, Mr Bott," he went on, at the same time stepping down lightly into the launch and carefully stowing Aunt Jocelyn's shopping order. "Children, this is Mr Bott—of Friendly, Friendly, Friendly and Bott."

"We know him," muttered Brian a little ungraciously.

The enemy's features stiffened as he set eyes on the boy. But he nodded politely and stepped down after Uncle Joseph to take an upright seat in the very centre of the launch. "Mr Bott's coming back with us," explained Uncle Joseph, as he helped Ann aboard.

"That's obvious," muttered Brian, retreating into the bow and staring out across the water.

The presence of the Enemy spoiled the trip back up the river. The Carrick Roads were just as alive with breezy freedom; yachts heeled and danced in the rising wind; the river was just as rich with tranquil beauty. But all the while the launch chugged back towards Gill Creek, the two children sat biting back their anxiety in case the Enemy reported to Uncle Joseph on their escapade of the previous Monday. But the Enemy said nothing. He sat rigid and obviously oblivious to the wooded beauty all around. Now the launch was edging into

the quiet smoothness of Gill Creek, sending one or
two nervous herons flapping away across the silky
waters. The quaint towers of the Folly peeped
shyly above the trees.

"Just a quick survey, Matthews," snapped the
Enemy, as soon as they were all safely ashore. This
was the first time the children had heard anyone
use their uncle's surname. They stood aghast as the
Enemy strutted across the lawn and began to give
voice to the most outrageous comments in between
making precise jottings in a black notebook.

"We'll bulldoze a road down through here!"
He was pointing vaguely towards the green beauty
of the woods which formed such a perfect background to the peaceful setting of the Folly. "Make
it big enough for motor-coaches to get down to the
river."

Ann and Brian exchanged dismayed glances.
Uncle Joseph said nothing. He stood looking old,
his shoulders bent, his face pale.

"Those bushes will have to go," the Enemy was
saying, his arm sweeping like a vandal's scythe towards the gorgeous banks of giant rhododendrons
which nestled close to the river bank.

"We'll lay a car park there. Nice solid area of
tarmac. Have to build a new concrete pier. A
couple of juke-boxes in the house and we'll have
the trippers swarming up the river from Falmouth.
Make a wonderful riverside cafe. Regular gold
mine. Pity you can't afford to buy the place yourself, Matthews. Think of all the money you've been
losing over the years when you could have been
cashing in on this ideal situation. Nothing like a

bit of free scenic beauty to get the holidaymakers parting with their money."

Ann had heard enough. Whitefaced, she blundered into the house. Aunt Jocelyn sat at the table, her head in her hand. She sat up quickly as Ann came in, and blinked back a tear.

"What's happening, Aunt?" Ann was not far from tears herself.

"We didn't want to worry you with this, me dears. Didn't want to spoil your holiday."

"Please tell us, Aunt," put in Brian, who was looking unusually concerned and serious.

Aunt Jocelyn sighed. "Not much to tell, really. You know Uncle Joseph worked for Lord Treloar, who died six months back. Well, heavy death duties mean that the estates have to be sold and that includes the Folly. We tried to raise the money to save the place from the sort of fate that Mr Bott has in mind. But not a hope. £50,000 is the asking price. Way beyond our savings."

Ann remembered the scribbling on the *Zoomman Comic*. Everything clicked into place. "But where will you and Uncle live?"

"Don't worry about us. They have to rehouse us. We've been offered a council house in Falmouth."

"A council house," sniffed Ann. "After *this*." She glanced out of the window at the perfect scene framed in the lattice.

"It's the birds and things that your uncle is concerned about," sighed her aunt. "What will happen to them with the place swarming with noise and rubbish?"

Just then Uncle Joseph came wearily into the

room. "He's gone," he announced thankfully "He's walking back to the Big House to spend the night."

"That sold as well?" asked Ann, for no particular reason.

"That's right," said her uncle. "London firm bought it. Going to turn it into a country club. Sounds a bit happier than the fate in store for the poor old Folly. Juke-boxes, motor-coaches!" He glanced despairingly around the comfortable room.

"But we can pray," he said at last. A hush filled the room. "Dear Lord, we do not wish to be selfish," he began, "but it seems almost sacrilege to ruin a place which you have made so beautiful." Here he paused for what seemed to the children a long, long while. The steady tick of the clock measured out the silence. "But help us, O Lord," he went on at last. "Help us to bow to Your will, whatever that will may be."

"Amen," added Ann fervently. She could hear her aunt crying softly. "It does seem wrong," she mused, as the children made their way back towards their camp. "Wrong that a place God has made so beautiful should be messed up."

"And just so's that old Enemy can make a lot of money," added Brian. He broke off a rotten end of a branch and hurled it out across the placid waters. He could never remember being so cross about anything in his life before.

As the day died slowly in the west, Ann toyed with the idea of building a beach fire. But somehow the news about the fate in store for Ferryman's Folly had spoiled the fun of the holiday. After cooking a couple of that morning's catch, the children drifted up into the Den and flopped into the deck-chairs. Brian did not even have the heart to have a go on the telescope.

On the far shore the Alien's fire flickered into life. Ann watched the distant dancing flames without particular interest. They now had a much bigger problem than trying to get to know the Aliens. She sat racking her brains for some way in which she could help. But no feasible plan suggested itself.

"We could kidnap the Enemy," put in Brian, after a long silence. "Kidnap him and force him not to sell the Folly."

Ann could not even raise a smile at the stupidity of this suggestion. The black hand of despair seemed to be pushing her deeper and deeper into despondency.

Taking his sister's silence for agreement, Brian enlarged on his idea. "We could row him up the river 'n threaten to drown him if he don't do what we say." Brian's look was supposed to be fierce. It was funny enough to stir his sister to a smile.

"I'm turning in now," she yawned. "Up early this morning. You better come, too."

"Aw, just five minutes," Brian muttered, springing up and grasping the telescope. "I'm not a bit tired."

Ann paused at the door. "Make sure it is just five minutes, then," she warned.

Brian was not listening. He was carefully focusing the telescope towards the distant dark bank. "Easy, it would be," he was musing. "Easy as pie——"

Ann dropped off to sleep as soon as she snuggled down into the warm folds of the sleeping-bag. It was a deep, undisturbed, dreamless sleep—at least, it was undisturbed for half-an-hour. What woke her she would never know. It was not a noise. More of an absence of a noise. More of a vague feeling that Brian was not safely in bed in the tent next door. She kept her eyes closed and tried to drift away from the tug of anxiety back down into the peace of sleep. It proved impossible.

Dragging her dressing-gown tight round her shoulders, she wriggled out of the tent, a torch clutched in one hand. She shone it through the flap of the other tent. An empty sleeping-bag lay twisted on the groundsheet. She glanced towards the boathouse. It was not yet really dark.

"I'll give him five minutes," she was muttering, as she trudged up the wooden steps, her slippers flapping on each step.

"Why you not in bed?" she demanded in her superior voice, at the same time flinging open the door. No answer. The dim interior stood empty. Grumbling to herself, she turned back down the steps and flashed the torch back towards the trees. Nothing. A sudden sinking feeling filled her. She hurried round the boathouse and scrambled up onto the slipway. Just as she had thought. The *Lady Peregrine* was missing.

Ann stared out across the deserted river. The ripple of the ebbing tide filled the night. On the far shore the Alien's fire flickered dimly. But of Brian there was neither sight nor sound.

CHAPTER NINE

MAN-NAPPING!

Brian's plan had formed quickly in his mind. He had heard his uncle say the Enemy would be staying the night at the Big House. As his sister tramped off down the steps and across to her tent, he attempted to use the telescope to pick out the outline of the chimneys of Penrye House above the trees on the far bank, but the light proved too poor.

"Dead easy," he murmured. "Just a simple case of man-napping and all Uncle's troubles would be over."

After giving Ann a little time to settle down in her tent, he crept from the boathouse and around to the *Lady Peregrine*. Launching the dingy was not easy single-handed, nor was the handling of the oars. Brian was not taking to the sea with the ease of his older sister. But at last he managed to navigate the crossing and felt the bow scrape lightly on the pebbles of the far shore. He took particular care to land as far as possible from the flickering flames of the Aliens' fire. Not that there was any sign of those other four campers. Their fire burned low on an empty beach.

Brian had landed as near as possible opposite to

where he remembered the Big House chimneys peeped from the wood. Securing the dingy to a bending branch, he slipped away into the trees. Once again the climb was steep and filled with much scrambling and slipping and barking of the shins. Night noises filled the woods with mystery. Tonight there was no moon to light the shadows. Heavy clouds darkened the sky. Brian was glad he had grabbed his duffel coat before hurrying from the boathouse; the night felt damp with the threat of rain.

In fact, Brian felt the first spots touch his face as he at last burst from the trees and found himself on the edge of a darkened sweep of lawn leading away to the stark silhouette of a large, rambling mansion which dominated the skyline above him. Light filtered from one ground floor window and drew the boy across the grass and up the hill. He approached cautiously. The room was large and oak-panelled. At the shining table which dominated the centre of the room sat two familiar figures: the Enemy and the lady in the hat. For the first time this formidable figure sat bare-headed. In a deep, comfortable chair at the far end of the room, her husband lay deep in his customary sleep. The table lay scattered with papers. The Enemy seemed to be reading from a document covered with tiny print; the lady listened with shrewd attention. Outside in the shadows Brian frowned. He had hoped to catch the Enemy on his own.

The boy drew close under the shelter of a spreading tree. Now the rain was falling steadily. The rising wind stirred and moaned through the creaking branches. Brian waited and waited till the cold and damp began to seep through the folds of the duffel coat. Keeping well away from the light he shuffled, stamped, and flapped his arms. Still the figures in the brightly lit room continued their late night business. The lady's husband snored blissfully on.

And while the Enemy worked and the lady listened and Brian waited, Ann had got herself into an unpleasant position. When she knew Brian was gone, she had hurried back to her tent and struggled quickly into her clothes. Pulling on her duffel coat, she raced back to the shore. Here she paused and thought quickly. Since the Enemy had decided to walk back to Penrye House, it was obviously possible to reach the place on foot from the Folly. She had immediately cottoned on to the fact that Brian was attempting to put his wild plan into practice, and she knew that she must get to him before he got himself into serious trouble. He had not even bothered to take his life-jacket when he had gone creaking off across the water.

Like a ghost flitting from tree to tree, the girl slipped back along the path to Ferryman's Folly. She crept by. A light on downstairs told her that her aunt and uncle were still up. Now she was climbing the unexplored path up past the house where she had seen the Enemy vanish that first time he had come by the Folly. Over the brow of the hill through the woods ran the track. Then it divided, one path dipping down into the trees at the other side of the hill, one running along the summit. She hesitated just long enough to flick her torch beam around the surrounding trees. An ancient signpost stood rotting slowly at the fork. St Mawes, indicated one arrow. Penrye, announced the arrow which pointed through the wood.

Slithering and sliding, Ann hurried down the path. The night was growing darker each moment. Just as she reached the impassable waters of Ruan Creek the rain began to fall. A small stone jetty flanked the shore. There were one or two rusty mooring rings but no boats. How did folk get across? Ann pondered the question anxiously. She was not to know that there was a rowing-boat kept at the crossing for visitors to the Big House but that at this particular moment it lay moored on the far bank where the Enemy had left it after rowing awkwardly across earlier in the evening.

"Hello, there!" Ann's clear voice rang out across the creek. She thought perhaps there might be another ferry-boat. "Ahoy. Is there a boat?" Surprisingly enough, after a slight pause there came an answer in the form of a small rowing-boat creaking slowly towards her across the water. She waited, all pleased and unsuspecting. As the rain grew thicker, she failed to recognise the approaching dingy as the *Lady Peregrine* or to identify the two dim figures crouched low over an oar apiece. The first indication she had that something was wrong was when one of the figures came leaping ashore and she found herself in the grips of the smallest Alien boy.

"Aw—you're hurting," she gasped, at the same time kicking the boy hard and low on the shins. His grip loosened and Ann would have wriggled free if the bigger boy had not come to his brother's aid.

"Got yu'!" he announced triumphantly. "You're our prisoner. Now in the boat." The voice was imperious with command.

Ann felt flushed and annoyed. She would have refused to comply except for the fact that she was extremely anxious to discover what had happened to Brian. She shrugged and stepped aboard to sit saying nothing as the dingy slipped back across the rain-swept creek. She pulled up her duffel coat hood and began to wonder what the two rough boys had done with Brian.

But, of course, Brian was perfectly all right, and at that moment was still waiting outside the Big House. He was now a little more hopeful of achieving his end since the Enemy and the lady had now left the room. If only he could get inside he might be able to get the Enemy on his own. He moved in close and examined the window. It was of the french door variety and he rattled the catch hopefully. It was firmly bolted on the inside. He was about to turn away when he noticed that the lady's sleepy husband had popped open his eyes and was staring dreamily across the room at him. It was a pleasant face. The stout figure rose from the enveloping chair and he came swaying across the room. Brian would have turned and bolted in normal circumstances, but the man's face was wreathed in a welcoming smile. The french door swung open and the man was beckoning him inside.

"Nasty night for you boys to be out." The voice was dreamy. "Come on into the warm."

"Thanks, mister," said an astonished Brian. He squelched into the room and stood shaking raindrops over the sleek, white carpet.

"That's a fine little fellow," said the man, returning to his chair and sinking back into a pleasant stupor, as Brian tramped a muddy line of footprints across to the door. It was opened into a wide hall, with a massive crystal chandelier dipping low over the broad sweep of impressive staircase.

"Wonder where the Enemy went?" muttered Brian. He hesitated and glanced upstairs. Gone to bed? It seemed likely. Brian's dirty brown footprints made an interesting addition to the pattern on the expensive stair carpet. A long, echoing gallery opened off at the head of the staircase. Brian made a tiny figure as he tip-toed between the dark oil paintings that linked the oak walls. He glanced at the doors as he passed. Who could tell which was the Enemy's room? Brian had never seen so many doors in his life before.

Then he heard the singing—if you could call it singing. A shrill, ear-splitting whine filtered from a half-open door near the end of the corridor. The sound of splashing proclaimed it was a bathroom. Brian stuck his head around the door. Success! The Enemy, in vest and pyjama trousers, was bent double over a wash-basin, covered in soap, water, and lather, singing like a mistuned starling.

"You gotta come with me." At Brian's stark announcement, the song died and the Enemy whirled round, his eyes boggling. He was an interesting sight.

"You!" he croaked. "Not again."

"You gotta come back with me." Brian repeated the simple statement. He could think of little else to say.

"Ah, of course." The Enemy looked happier. "Your uncle sent you. There's trouble at Ferryman's Folly?"

"There's trouble at Ferryman's Folly, all right," said Brian significantly, thinking of all the nasty things the Enemy had planned for the delightful spot.

"Trouble," repeated the Enemy, thinking of fire and deathwatch beetle and floods. "I'll come at once. Just wait till I get dressed."

A happy, contented Brian drifted back to the stairs. He eyed the long, sleek bannisters with an expert eye. Kidnapping was even easier than he had imagined. He straddled the tempting rails and zoomed down into the hall to fall into a jumbled heap just as the lady, still without her hat, came sweeping in from another room. She contemplated the wet figure without comment and stepped carefully over him. Vaguely she recognised that impish face. Must be something to do with the servants. She carried on into the room where her husband lay snoring sweetly. She prodded him back to consciousness.

"Who is that boy?" She crossed to the window and peered out into the driving rain.

"What boy, dear?" Her husband blinked owlishly.

"The wet boy in the hall."

"One of our little nephews, isn't he, dear? Freddy or Tom?"

"Don't be silly, dear," she replied evenly. "Surely you have been awake long enough since you've been here to recognise your own nephews."

"All little boys look alike to me," yawned her husband. He was beginning to feel sleepy. His head drooped onto his chest.

The lady made a clicking noise with her tongue and strode back into the hall. The Enemy was just swinging open the massive front door. Wind and rain swirled into the hall. The boy stood, all innocent, still wrapped in his long, damp duffel coat.

"And where might you be off to, Mr Bott?"

"Urgent message," panted the Enemy. "Ferryman's Folly's on fire!"

Brian blinked. He had never actually said *that*. But somehow the Enemy seemed to have inferred it from the boys urgent manner.

"Fire?" The lady's eyebrows arched. "And the house still belongs to me?"

"And not fully insured," put in the Enemy with a gulp. "Not to todays prices."

"Then I'd best come with you, Bott." Without further ado the lady swept back through the door to rouse her husband. "Get your coat, dear. The place is on fire!"

"Fire!" the sleeper sprung from the chair and tore out into the hall. Snatching up the phone he began to bellow down the mouthpiece. The Enemy and Brian stood staring at him, open-mouthed. He caught the Enemy's eye and shouted encouragingly. "Don't worry, Bott, old man. Soon have the Force here. All hands to the pumps, eh?"

"George!" The lady came sailing back into the

hall, wearing a mackintosh like a small bell-tent. "The fire is not here but at Ferryman's Folly. Still, perhaps it would do no harm to get the Brigade out."

Brian swallowed hard as he heard her dialling 999. He was sure he had never actually *said* the Folly was ablaze.

Out into the rain-swept night marched the party. Brian took the lead, the Enemy grumbling close behind, the lady marching with resolute determination, and finally her husband cheerfully yawning his way along in the rear.

"There *is* a path," sniffed the Enemy, as Brian led them down into the trees.

"But I got me own boat," called back Brian, who was having serious doubts about the entire man-napping expedition at this stage. The extra folk who had tailed on introduced problems. Could he get them all aboard the *Lady Peregrine*? The lady was huge. More Ocean Queen size than dingy passenger material. Like a miniature herd of elephants they crashed down through the wet undergrowth and dripping trees. At the beach a new problem presented itself, for, of course, the *Lady Peregrine* had gone.

"Never mind," snapped the Enemy impatiently. "We'll use our own boat."

He took the lead along the squelching beach towards the point Ann had wanted to cross. On this shore, at the end of a path obviously leading up to the Big House, was chained a heavy dingy. The Enemy produced a key and unpadlocked the moorings.

"Have to do this to keep those two nephews of yours getting their hands on her."

The man-napping plan was definitely going astray. Brian perched in the rear of the rowing-boat as the Enemy pulled awkwardly across the river, and thought desperately. The boat lay low in the water, the combined weight of the lady and her husband proving a burden hard to be borne! With a shudder they hit the mudbank and stuck fast. A normally laden boat would have cleared it.

"What's wrong?" The lady's voice was threatening.

The Enemy did not trouble to reply. He stretched unsteadily to his lanky legs and grasping an oar with both hands attempted to shove the rowing boat free. Sluggishly she shifted, caught again, then came free with a rush. The Enemy had to make a quick decision. Either he hung onto the oar and ended up in the creek or lost the oar and stayed aboard. He chose the latter course. The boat drifted sideways with the ebbing tide, leaving the lost oar fast in the mudbank.

The Enemy made frantic attempts to progress with one remaining oar but managed only to spin in aimless circles. In the grip of the fast retreating tide the rowing boat was borne down-river. The steady rain drenched down. Water ran from the end of the Enemy's nose.

Despite the wet, Brian grinned. He had made it. Two man-nappings and a woman-napping. As he said, it was easy!

CHAPTER TEN

THE MUD THICKENS

As the *Lady Peregrine* creaked across the river to the opposite dark bank, Ann listened to the Aliens' chatter and soon gathered that the oldest Alien was Fred and the youngest Tom.

"Hey, you girls! Come quick," called Tom, leaping out onto the beach as soon as the dingy's keel scrunched on the pebbles. "We've nabbed a prisoner."

There was a crashing and scrambling from the murky undergrowth and out of the night came the two Alien girls, shrouded in duffel coats and flashing torches in Ann's direction.

"Oh, it's the girl from the green tents," came the voice of the older girl as her probing beam momentarily dazzled Ann. "What are you doing with her?"

"She's our prisoner, of course, Sue." Fred came leaping lightly ashore his face bright with triumph.

"But what's she done?" broke in the voice of the younger Alien girl, a little anxiously.

"Done?" echoed Tom. "Done? You don't have to do anything to get captured by pirates!"

"So you're pirates, are you?" Ann tried to sound

very grown-up and unimpressed by these childish games.

" 'Course we are," muttered Tom. "Anyone can *see* we are pirates."

Ann peered at him through the darkness. He looked just like any other small boy.

The girl Sue spoke again. "Don't you think this is going too far?" Her voice sounded brim-full of doubt. "I mean, borrowing a boat is one thing, and even raiding their camp was not so bad; but capturing one of them——"

"Too soft, you girls," growled Fred in his best pirate-like voice.

"Well, Pat and I are not going to play your silly old game any more," murmured Sue, taking her sister's hand and preparing for an angry show-down with her two brothers.

"That's right," confirmed Pat, the youngest Alien, with a toss of her damp curls. "Pretending is fine—but capturing a real girl is going too far."

Ann felt a warm glow despite the wind and rain as she listened to this spirited display. Here were a couple of Aliens who would make super friends.

"We didn't hurt her." Tom's voice sounded sulky.

"You did, too," put in Ann, enjoying this chance to get her own back. "Twisted my arm, you did."

"An' she kicked me," murmured Tom. "Didn't she, Fred?"

But Fred did not want to expand the argument. He muttered something about girls and turned his attention back to the dingy. Ann moved over and was soon chatting merrily with the two friendly Alien girls. Tom turned away shamefaced to help his brother. They had landed a little way downstream of the still flickering fire, at a spot where a narrow inlet opened off the creek and edged a little way into the trees. The *Lady Peregrine* had been tucked away just out of sight in this inlet. It was impossible to shove her very far into the trees, since the ebbing tide had reduced the channel to a trickle. It was here the pirates lurked with their prisoner when Brian and his 'kidnapped' party came crashing down through the trees further up-river.

It was Tom who first noticed the runaway rowing-boat with its distinguished crew. The girls were still giggling and enjoying a growing friendship. Fred was pretending to be busy fiddling with the *Lady Peregrine*, while Tom just drifted out onto the dark beach to fling a few frustrated stones into the murky water.

"A boat," he murmured, as he noticed the dark shape slipping by in midstream, held fast in the swift flowing tide. He flicked on his torch and probed the beam out across the water. An immediate shout echoed back across the creek. "Help! Help! We are drifting out to sea. Save us at once— do you hear?"

Tom's heart missed a beat. "Aunt Matilda!" he gasped beneath his breath. Already he was withdrawing silently into the shadow of the trees. Blundering back to the *Lady Peregrine*, he silenced the continual chatter of the girls with a hoarse stage whisper. "It's Aunt Matilda!"

His announcement produced immediate silence.

"Out looking for us, you mean?" Fred's voice came at last, strangely subdued.

"Don't think she's actually looking for us," answered Tom. "She shouted something about drifting out to sea. There's a whole boat full of 'em. Uncle George—and that man Bott—and that boy."

"Brian?" put in Ann quickly.

Fred sniffed. "They can't be really drifting out to sea. The sea's miles away. The worst that could happen to 'em is that they drift out into the deep waters of the Fal."

"What if they capsize or sink or something?" Sue sounded anxious.

"We must rescue them," added Pat.

"Not likely," said Fred at once. "Could be a trap. You know how Aunt Matilda said we were not to leave our tents at night. She's just trying to catch us out."

"I expect she went prying round our tents, found we were not there and decided to set a trap for us," hissed Tom.

"Nonsense!" snapped Sue, "Come on, girls. If these boys are scared, we'll do it on our own."

"You can't row a boat," said Tom sulkily.

"But I can," said Ann, triumphantly. "If Brian is on that boat with your aunt, I've got to get him back before my aunt and uncle find out that we are out of our tents at night."

As the three determined girls advanced towards the *Lady Peregrine*, Fred shrugged and admitted defeat. "All right, then. We'll all go."

"Bit of a squeeze, it'll be," muttered Tom ungraciously.

"Have to leave *you* behind, then," put in Sue.

But no-one had to be left. The *Lady Peregrine* just about managed to hold all five children and at last with much pushing and shoving and grunting they launched off on a voyage of rescue. By now, wind and rain howled down the valleys, tearing at the trees, filling the night with wild voices. Soon the retreating tide gripped the dingy and she was hurling along in pursuit of Brian and his kidnapped crew, who by now had been swallowed up in the night. Ann crouched with Sue in the bow, their torches like searchlight beams sweeping the waters ahead of them.

"There they are!" squealed the two girls in unison, as they sighted a dark shape which seemed to be stationary in the ebbing tide. At the very same moment came the sickening jolt as the *Lady Peregrine* grounded on a mudbank. Dismayed, the children pushed on the oars, rocked the dingy, and did everything they could think of to get free; but with every passing second the retreating tide was leaving them more and more firmly stranded on a long, low mudbank. Just fifty yards away the other rowing-boat crew were attempting similar and equally futile tactics to release their vessel.

"We'll be here all night," said Fred gloomily. "No getting off till the morning tide."

Sue explored their surroundings with the help of her torch. Already the soft, squelching mud was appearing all round them. They lay some hundred yards from the wooded shore, a hundred yards of deep mud and slimy pools before the narrow, pebbled beach began. The other rowing-boat lay a little further down-river and about the same distance from the boathouse and something like a mile from Ferryman's Folly. The fearsome figure of Aunt Matilda dominated the other boat. She began to call through the rain.

"Freddy? Thomas? Is that you?"

"We're all here, Aunt," shouted back Sue. "We've come to rescue you."

"Rescue?" Aunt Matilda's voice competed with the wind. "And how do you propose to do it?" The question whirled unanswered in the wind. The Enemy sat crouched, water running off the end of his nose, shivering away the seconds and muttering something about the Folly being lost through fire and flame. Brian grinned to himself as he listened. On a night like this, any self-respecting fire would dowse itself in disgust. Only Uncle George seemed really content. He had pulled his raincoat up round his neck, dragged his hat down over his eyes, laid a practised head on the gunwhale and retreated into the snug security of sleep.

In the other boat, Ann sighed. By morning they would all be drenched through to the bone. Possibly they would all contract pneumonia. She remembered her mother's warning about sleeping in damp beds and of always changing out of damp clothes as soon as possible. She was glad her mother could not see her at this moment. The rain increased in intensity. The great black clouds seemed to be weeping with fury. Suddenly the entire scene was lit by a stark white light. For a second every-

thing stood out weird and distorted, like an over-
exposed picture; then the darkness snapped shut
again and almost at once came the crack and rumble
of the following thunder.

Ann paled; she was not too keen on thunder
storms at the best of times. She felt a small hand
reach out and grab hers. It was Pat the smallest
Alien.

"It's all right," she soothed. "Only a bit of
thunder." She immediately began to feel better.

"Hey, that's really great!" enthused Tom, as
the next flash lit the surrounding hills. He stood up
in the boat and cheered as the thunder broke.

"Sit down," fussed Sue, trying to sound brave
and confident.

"Just 'lectric sparks," sulked her brother, flop-
ping back into the wet boat.

Across in the other boat, Brian decided it was
time to put his plan into practice. Things had not
gone exactly the way he had expected but there
still might be hope of getting the Enemy to change
his mind over the fate of the Folly.

"Mr Bott, sir." He had decided to be very polite
and to use the Enemy's real name. The Enemy
answered with a potent sneeze, full of rich promise
of a fast-approaching cold. "You didn't oughter do
it."

"You're right, boy," put in Aunt Matilda. "He
should learn to use a handkerchief."

"No—not that," piped up Brian impatiently.
"The Folly, I mean."

"Burned!" groaned the Enemy dramatically.
"Razed to the ground, while we sit helpless."

Brian sighed. This was going to be more difficult than he had imagined "It's not on fire at all——" he began, but Aunt Matilda cut him short.

"Why, then, are we out here, boy?"

The Enemy sneezed again. "Burned! Money up in smoke!" he muttered.

"But—but——" Brian stuttered when he was really excited.

"But nothing, boy," insisted Aunt Matilda. "Just sit quiet and hope for a speedy rescue."

Brian sighed and lapsed into silence. The whole thing had become too complicated for him and he felt suddenly tired, very tired. His head dropped onto his shoulder. Slowly he tipped forward against the snoring figure of Uncle George. The storm had passed overhead. The lightning flashes grew less frequent, the thunder less violent.

Ann felt growing relief. But still the rain swept down across the two boats and the cold damp chilled her bones.

"Couldn't you wade through the mud, Fred?" put in Pat.

"Dunno," shrugged her brother.

"Could be dangerous," put in Sue quickly. "Some of those pools look awful deep."

"We oughter do *something*," said Tom. "I'm freezing to death."

"We could pray." Ann made the suggestion hesitantly, shyly.

"Like in Sunday school?" Tom sounded interested.

"I was reading last night where it says, 'Call upon Me in the day of trouble: I will deliver thee',' went on Ann.

"That in the Bible?" said Tom.

" 'Course it is," put in Fred.

"We're certainly in trouble," mused Pat.

"Up to our necks," agreed Sue.

And so they closed their eyes, while the rain continued to fall and the wind to creak and moan through the distant trees.

"Heavenly Father," began Ann, "You can see the sort of trouble we have got ourselves into. Please send us help——"

She paused and tried to think of something more. The sound of Mr Bott sneezing drifted over to them.

In the following silence, Ann added a private prayer the others could not hear. "Please, Lord, help me to become a real Christian when all this is over." She felt her spirits rise after she had breathed this silent request. Deep inside she realised that God answered the prayers of people who were sincerely prepared to let Him control their lives. Out loud, she just added. "We ask this for Jesus' sake, Amen."

A little circle of 'Amens' added their sincere agreement to the plea for God's help.

Ann felt better already. The rain and wind were as wild as ever but she thrust both hands into her pockets and felt warm despite the storm. Her fingers closed round the cold shape of the whistle her uncle had given her.

"We're saved!" she cried. "Why didn't I think of it before?"

In the other boat the Enemy sneezed once more,

his nose red and damp. Uncle George and Brian
snoozed happily, and Aunt Matilda sat fretting and
fuming beneath her giant mackintosh. She blinked
and peered out through the driving rain as the first
desperate shrill notes of the whistle rose and fell
above the storm.

CHAPTER ELEVEN

DESPERATE MEASURES

Uncle Joseph was angry, anxious, and mystified all at one and the same time. At the first spot of rain that tapped the Folly windows, Aunt Jocelyn had sent him hurrying off in the direction of the green tents with orders to bring the children back in out of the approaching storm. Of course, the tents were empty, the *Lady Peregrine* missing, and Uncle Joseph fuming.

"Oh dear, oh dear," fussed Aunt Jocelyn, as soon as her husband returned with this unwelcome news. "And I thought that Ann was much too sensible a girl to go out on the river at night."

She remained anxious at the living-room window as her husband donned his oil-skins and once more hurried out into the night. For a moment he toyed with the idea of taking the motor-launch; but he knew the tide was falling fast and the launch needed fairly deep water. Finally, settling for a flat-bottomed punt which was ideal in shallow water, he rowed swiftly off towards the boathouse promontory. Rounding the point he headed up Ruan Creek. It seemed the obvious direction the children would take. And so he slipped quietly up-river, unnoticed, at the very moment Ann and the Aliens were arguing in the secrecy of the hidden inlet and Brian was leading his party down through the trees from the Big House. He rowed far beyond the crossing point to the Big House and so missed the faulty oarsmanship of the Enemy.

At last Uncle Joseph decided to turn back. The ebbing tide had left him a narrow channel and he feared to go further in case he was stranded. Swinging the punt neatly round, he let the retreating waters bear him back down-river. Surely the children had not gone further up towards Ruan? Reaching the Big House landing-place, a sudden idea struck him. Perhaps Ann and Brian were visiting the other children in their camp high up on the hillside. He slid into the landing and was soon hurrying off through the trees. He skirted the lawn of the Big House, noticing how dark and empty the place looked. He ploughed through another wood and came out into the clearing. His powerful torchbeam picked out the two white tents. A distant flash of lightning was answered by a roll of thunder. He paused, stood stark still, listening. Was that the shrill call of a whistle? He hesitated, listening hard. There it was again, faint and distant. Somewhere out across the creek? As the shrill notes again rose plaintively above the storm, Uncle Joseph was off, panting and puffing his way back towards the spot where he had left his punt.

Back out towards the mouth of the creek, two well-soaked and stranded crews stared hopefully back towards the direction of Ferryman's Folly. Even Uncle George had abandoned his hobby long

enough to show some slight interest in the pos-
sibility of rescue. But the rescue came from the
opposite direction.

"Boat coming!" squealed Brian suddenly. He
pointed excitedly out towards the mouth of the
creek where the broad Fal lazed down towards the
sea. The rain had dropped to a sprinkle, only the
wind keeping up its full fury. Aunt Matilda peered
in the direction of the boy's pointing finger. Sure
enough, a red and green light, holding the dark
outline of a fair-sized launch, was nosing up the
creek, keeping expertly to the dredged centre
channel.

"Hey, there! Ahoy! Ahoy!" hailed Brian,
bounding up and down and rocking the rowing-
boat on its mud-bound keel.

"Come and rescue us at once!" added Aunt
Matilda with regal insistence.

Brian blinked as there was a flash from the
approaching vessel and a powerful searchlight
beam came leaping out across the mud-flats.

"Ahoy, there. You in trouble?" a booming
megaphone echoed across the creek.

"Trouble," fumed Aunt Matilda. "Do you think
we are enjoying ourselves stuck here like this?"

The engine note of the dimly-lit vessel changed
pitch and she hove to some fifty yards away across
the mud. A sudden flicker from the dying storm
played on her outline.

DOCKS FIRE SERVICE, read Brian. A crew of uni-
formed men stood staring across at them.

"We're on our way to a fire at Ferryman's Folly,"
boomed the microphone. Brian gulped as he

remembered the telephone message.

"Please do what you can to save *us* first," shouted Aunt Matilda. "We are cold and wet, and who knows what will happen to us if we don't get off before morning!"

There followed a shouting and bustling aboard the fire-fighting vessel as the crew prepared for the rescue.

"We'll have to use desperate measures," boomed the megaphone.

"Use whatever you like—only GET US OFF THIS MUD!" Aunt Matilda's voice rolled like thunder down the creek. The firemen were used to obeying orders and flew into action. The fire-boat kept in midstream, her tender ferrying the first firemen to the mudbanks. They wore great thigh-length rubber boots and plunged immediately into the mud. Squelching and struggling they came through the wet night, guided by the probe of the searchlight. Brian was the first to be carried to safety. A burly fireman, standing knee-deep in black mud, scooped the boy from the rowing-boat and began struggling back with him towards the waiting rescue boat.

"Hey! This is great," Brian squealed, as the strong arms of the fireman bore him high across the mud.

Aunt Matilda went next, fussing and ordering her way to safety in the wilting arms of two of the biggest firemen.

"Phew!" they gasped together, as they dropped her in an undignified heap into the tender. "Due for a course of dieting, aren't you, m'dear?" Aunt

Matilda gave them a haughty look and kept her comments to herself. After all, she mused, one *ought* to be grateful for being rescued, even if one's rescuers *were* a pair of ill-mannered, ill-bred fellows!

Uncle George came next; his was a relaxed, un-eventful journey. But when the Enemy's turn came, the only accident of the night spoiled an otherwise perfect rescue.

"D-do—b-be careful," bleated the solicitor, as the puniest of the firemen lifted his thin frame out of the rowing-boat.

"Safe as houses with me, chum," grinned the fireman. But, then, houses can and do fall down, blow up, burn to the ground, and suffer from any of a hundred and three fatal diseases, as the Enemy well knew from his professional dealings with real estate. Whether the fireman stumbled or the Enemy wriggled too much, no-one knew, and only the Enemy himself cared, and he chose never to reveal the secret. But whatever the cause, Mr Bott was dumped suddenly and unexpectedly into the thickest, blackest, squelchiest spot in the creek.

"Ugh! You need a bath, Bott," sniffed Aunt Matilda, as the mud-enslimed figure was at last dumped into the bottom of the tender. The Enemy sneezed seven times in quick succession.

After the tender had carried the first lot to safety, the rescue vessel chugged along opposite the second boat and the cheerful firemen soon had the five children safely taken off the stranded *Lady Peregrine*. The Fire Chief was about to give the order to head for the Folly when Uncle Joseph's faint hail reached them. He had raced back to his punt and swiftly rowed down the dredged channel from Ruan Creek and was now avoiding the mud-flats off the promontory.

"There be a fire at your place," called the Fire Chief, as he recognised the ferryman. "Here, catch a line. We'll give he a tow."

Uncle Joseph's heart leapt as he heard the word 'fire'; but he caught the tow rope neatly and allowed the fire-fighting vessel to tow him home.

Back at the Folly, Aunt Jocelyn stood peering out into the night. As soon as she heard and saw the boat approaching the ferryman's jetty, she hurried into the kitchen and put on the kettle. She came to the front door and flung it open just as two earnest, mud-spattered firemen came racing up the garden path unwinding a bulky hose.

"Ah, that's nice," she smiled. "You're just in time for coffee!"

Later that night, when all the confused explanations had been blurted out and the Fire Chief was first livid, then amused, then roaring with laughter, and the fire-fighting vessel had chugged off down-river, the rescued party sat thawing out and steaming before a roaring blaze. The Enemy had been bundled off to the bathroom, sneezing and twittering to himself. Everyone else sat huddled in borrowed, jumble-sale clothes several sizes too big.

"Of course, I *did* call the Fire Brigade," said Aunt Matilda brightly. "But I expected a road vehicle, not a boat."

"Can't get a road vehicle down to the Folly," put in Uncle Joseph. "Had to be a water-borne hose up from Falmouth Docks."

Ann exchanged a secret glance with Sue. She *knew* why it just had to be a boat. It had been an immediate answer to their prayers.

"I never actually *said* the Folly was on fire," muttered Brian to no-one in particular.

The flashing eye of Aunt Matilda fixed the boy. "Ah, now," she boomed. "This is the fine fellow who started all this rowing about in the rain, and I gather it was something to do with preventing us from selling this house."

"Well, a desperate situation seemed to call for desperate measures," answered a reddened Brian, remembering the words from an adventure book he had once read.

"So you kidnapped us all?" Aunt Matilda's eyes now twinkled.

"I never meant to kidnap *all* of you," put in Brian quickly. "Just the En—er—that Mr Bott. Then you *all* came traipsing along and——" His voice trailed off and he shrugged his shoulders.

"I think you're much too tired to talk about it all just now," smiled Aunt Jocelyn, exchanging a sly grin with Aunt Matilda. "Bed is the best place for us all just at this moment." She nodded towards the clock. It was one o'clock in the morning.

Soon Aunt Jocelyn was bustling about finding everyone a room and bed for what remained of the night. The weird design of the Folly offered a whole set of spare bedrooms which the hospitable aunt seldom had cause to use. She was rather pleased at this opportunity to dig out spare sheets and blankets and to settle every one of her visitors in a warm and comfortable bed.

Ann drifted off up her spiral stairs and thankfully undressed. But before tumbling into bed she just had to kneel and breathe a fervent thank-you to God for being rescued. She realised that even if her whistle blast had fetched Uncle Joseph he would never have been able to effect as immediate and effective a rescue as had the tough firemen. "All things worked together for good," she murmured as she flicked off the light and padded across to the bed. "Bed, you're my favourite friend," she continued as her head snuggled into the soft pillow. And so a day of adventure flitted softly away and smooth sleep filtered through her tired body. It seemed a whole lifetime since the harsh alarm had dragged her from the sleeping-bag at four-thirty in the morning.

Long and late into the next day slept the visitors to Ferryman's Folly. The sun was high and the river sparkling and full by the time Ann yawned from bed and peered out into a perfect morning. The wind and rain had long since fled, leaving Gill Creek at its smiling best. Uncle Joseph had since slipped down the creek to rescue the two rowing-boats as they lifted on the morning tide. Now they swung side by side at the jetty, reminding Ann that the two Alien girls were now her firm friends. Soon the boys would be as well.

In fact, by the time she sauntered downstairs for breakfast, Brian had already palled up with the boys and was planning a day's united adventure at the boathouse.

"Listen to this, Ann," Brian enthused. "We're

going to form a gang—all of us together—and then we're——"

He was cut short by the dramatic entrance of Aunt Matilda, who swept into the room followed by Uncle Joseph, Aunt Jocelyn, and a rather seedy-looking Mr Bott. "Just before you get too excited, young man," boomed the fearsome lady, her eyes devoid of smiles, "there are one or two points we must clear up about this disgraceful behaviour of you all last night!"

CHAPTER TWELVE

AUNT MATILDA'S PLAN

Mr Bott shambled into the room and huddled in a chair. He no longer looked that formidable foe who had won himself the title of Enemy. Now he was just a pathetic little man in the throes of a rapidly developing cold.

"You all right, Mr Bott, sir?" asked Ann shyly and sympathetically.

Mr Bott peered back at her with streaming eyes and sneezed into a large white handkerchief. "Not too good, my dear," he answered at last in a most friendly voice. "Should be in bed."

"Poor old Bott!" beamed Aunt Matilda. "He seems to have got himself the blame for all the Company's plans."

"He *was* going to chop down all the trees and kill all the birds and bring all those people tramping through the woods and have roads and——" burst out Brian; but Aunt Matilda cut him short.

"Whoa!" she laughed. "Poor old Bott was not going to do all those things personally. He was working for my husband. He only did what he was told, unfortunate man."

"Working for your husband?" Ann felt and

looked a little foolish.

"Of course," went on the Alien's aunt. She crossed to the window and looked out into the sunlit terrace. Her husband dozed gently in a convenient deck-chair. "Shrewd business man is my George," she announced proudly. "Managing Director of Holiday Holdings, the company who bought up Lord Treloar's estates."

"He doesn't half sleep a lot," broke in Brian. Ann frowned in his direction.

"He *thinks* a lot when he's asleep," explained Aunt Matilda brightly. "Some of his most profitable deals have been worked out from the depths of an arm-chair, at this very moment he's working on a take-over bid for a string of holiday camps right across Europe."

Brian sidled over to the window to stare out in amazement at the plump, slumbering features of Uncle George. "You'd never think so, just to look at him," he muttered.

"Well, of course, I do help him a little." A modest smile played in the depths of Aunt Matilda's firm grey eyes.

"And you hope to make a nice little profit out of Ferryman's Folly?" Uncle Joseph spoke softly.

Aunt Matilda did not reply at once. She moved away from the window and seemed to be surveying the room in some detail. "The Folly did not fit in with my—er—George's plans," she said at last. "The Big House will make a fine country club. You know the sort of thing—rest cures and a bit of fishing for city-weary businessmen."

"Would it be an awfully noisy place?" put in

Ann, thinking of the peace and seclusion of Ruan Creek.

"Noisy?" Aunt Matilda's eyebrows rose. "I should hope not. It will be a rather exclusive club for rather elderly executives. Shouldn't think there'll be a lot of noise."

"It wouldn't be a holiday camp, then?" Aunt Jocelyn sounded relieved.

"Hardly," echoed Aunt Matilda. "I—er— George would not dream of destroying a beautiful place like Penrye House by turning it into a holiday camp."

"But you don't mind destroying the Folly?" Uncle Joseph's voice was soft and sad.

Aunt Matilda stared at him before answering. "You must understand we had never set eyes on the Folly when we decided to sell. It was a decision of the Company Board. George and I hold majority shares and control the Board, of course."

She strolled back to the window and a great silence filled the room. The fate of the Folly rested on her words. "I—er—George could think of no useful purpose for a ferryman's cottage," she said at last. "Of course, we did not realise it would be anything like this." She stared out across the tranquillity of the beautiful creek with its soft, wooded hills. "Bott here suggested we would get a good price for it as a riverside cafe——"

"You *do* pay me to look after your financial interests," put in the deflated Enemy nervously.

"No-one's blaming *you*, Bott," went on Aunt Matilda. "Now I've seen the place, mind you——" She stopped and again the room seemed to hold its breath. "Now I've seen the place, it occurs to me it would make a really delightful escape cottage."

"Escape cottage?" echoed Brian.

"Hmmmm. A place to escape to for the weekend away from London. George works so hard, you know." She glanced affectionately towards her husband's slumbering form. "It would be a wonderful spot for George and me to get away from it all from time to time." She turned back from the window. "Of course, we'd need a reliable couple to keep the place running for us. Perhaps George could buy a little yacht and keep it moored out in the creek." She smiled towards Uncle Joseph and Aunt Jocelyn. "After all, the Company is only asking fifty thousand for the place. That sounds to me an excellent bargain and George could well afford it."

Aunt Jocelyn and Uncle Joseph exchanged a delighted smile. Ann felt her heart leap.

"Good old Uncle George!" shouted Brian, and the four Aliens joined in the cheering.

"Ah, now!" Aunt Matilda's glance fell on her nephews and nieces. "There is still the matter of being out of your tents at night and of stealing a rowing-boat and of——"

"We *were* trying to rescue you," offered Tom in a small voice. The other three looked sheepish.

"Humph," said their aunt. It was a vague expression which at that moment could have meant anything. "Humph. Perhaps a little stopping of pocket-money would cover the crime."

"'Spect so," muttered Tom. The other three grinned, happy to have escaped so lightly.

Their aunt turned away quickly so they would not see the twinkle in her eye. "Now then, Mr Matthews, would you show me over the gardens and river."

Uncle Joseph was delighted to do just that.

"Come on, Mr Bott," beamed Aunt Matilda. "You're my legal adviser. A little look round this beauty spot will do you a world of good." Mr Bott rose and followed obediently. He paused at the door and looked back at Mrs Matthews and the children.

"I'm glad, really," he shrugged. "My job's not an easy one, you know." He smiled at Brian. "Quite good fun last night, wasn't it?" He pulled out his handkerchief, sneezed rather loudly, giggled a little foolishly, and then hurried out after Aunt Matilda.

Ann and Brian looked at each other and laughed. Outside on the terrace they could hear Aunt Matilda explaining loudly: "Of course, it all depends on whether I can persuade George to agree. He may not take to a quiet place like this." As the footsteps echoed away down the garden path they could hear Uncle George snoring contentedly in the morning sunshine.

"Can we go off to the boathouse now?" piped up Brian. His face was an eager question-mark.

"You have a little punishment coming your way, too, young man," answered Aunt Jocelyn. "You know you should not have gone off like that."

Brian looked hurt. "B—but I was doing it to save the Folly."

Aunt Jocelyn hid her smile. "Go on, then, off

with you." She was talking to an empty space. Brian was already half-way down the garden path with the four Aliens on his tail.

Ann stayed behind. "I'm ever so glad, Aunt," she smiled.

"I know." Ann felt a deep contentment in her heart. "Aunt," she went on shyly. "I want to really dedicate my life to the Lord Jesus. Do I have to wait until we go to church on Sunday?"

"Of course not, my dear," smiled Aunt Jocelyn. "You can do it right now. The Bible explains that the day of salvation is always today."

Together they knelt by the sunny window. The gentle cooing of the doves in the woods behind the Folly filtered in with the sunshine.

"Heavenly Father," Ann found herself praying, "I thank You for sending the Lord Jesus to die for me on the cross. May his blood wash me clean from sin, and please, Lord, give me a new life and make me a real Christian."

Her aunt added a gentle prayer for God to guide and give Ann strength to tell other people about her decision to follow the Lord Jesus.

"Now run along and really enjoy the rest of your holiday with your new friends," said Aunt Jocelyn, as they rose happily to their feet. "And tell them they can all come along to church with us on Sunday."

"That'll be great," enthused Ann. She left the Folly and strolled down the garden path. Aunt Matilda was out on the Ferryman's jetty.

"Exactly what sort of yacht would you advise George to get?" she heard her asking Uncle Joseph.

Mr Bott smiled at the girl as she took the path through the rhododendron bushes and along the river towards the old boathouse. She wondered if the green tents would be all right after the rain. The river shone with beauty between its rich green banks that climbed away towards a deep blue sky.

"The lines have fallen to me in pleasant places," she found herself repeating. A heron came flapping lazily down the creek to settle in the shallows close under the bank. Ann paused to watch him stand motionless on his long legs in the rippling water. At least the wild-life would now be safe from holiday disturbance. The country club planned by Aunt Matilda sounded a peaceful sort of place, with tired old businessmen like Uncle George dozing all over the place.

The deep contentment of the creek as it basked in the warm sunshine seemed to fill the girl's heart with joy. As a new-born Christian she was standing on the brink of a new life. In the distance she heard the happy shouts of the other children and felt an immediate urge to share with them the secret of her new happiness. Now she was skipping along the winding path. At the promontory she hesitated and glanced back towards the Folly. The curious twin towers caught the sun and winked at her above the trees. Ann smiled. The Folly seemed to be saying thank you. Reluctantly she turned away and glanced down towards the boathouse. The twin green tents looked no worse for wear.

"Come on, Annee!" Brian's shout drifted up through the trees. They had already lit a driftwood fire. The four Aliens waved their welcome. Ann

broke into a run down the slight slope to the beach.
Ahead stretched more than three weeks of glorious
holiday and a whole lifetime of adventure and
excitement!